HEROES OF CHINA'S NEW ERA

THE CHALLENGES AND GLORY

The Journey of the Chinese Women's Volleyball Team

By Ma Yin

Translated by Wu Jie

China Intercontinental Press   CHINA YOUTH PUBLISHING GROUP

图书在版编目（CIP）数据

荆棘与荣耀：新时代女排奋斗记：英文 / 马寅著；吴杰译 .
-- 北京：五洲传播出版社，2021.1
（“新时代的中国人”丛书 . 第二辑）
ISBN 978-7-5085-4599-8

Ⅰ. ①荆… Ⅱ. ①马… ②吴… Ⅲ. ①纪实文学－中国－当代－英文
Ⅳ. ① I25

中国版本图书馆 CIP 数据核字 (2021) 第 214390 号

“新时代的中国人”丛书

出 版 人：关 宏
技术审校：梁自明

荆棘与荣耀：新时代女排奋斗记

著 者：马 寅
英文翻译：吴 杰
策划编辑：张美景
责任编辑：张美景
封面设计：谢敬一
装帧设计：杨 平 蒲建霖

出版发行：五洲传播出版社
地 址：北京市海淀区北三环中路 31 号生产力大楼 B 座 7 层
邮 编：100088
发行电话：010-82005927，82007837
网 址：http://www.cicc.org.cn http://www.thatsbooks.com
承 印 者：中煤（北京）印务有限公司
版 次：2022 年 9 月第 1 版第 1 次印刷
开 本：787×1092 mm 1/16
印 张：16.25
字 数：155 千字
定 价：119.00 元

PREFACE

The Spirit of the Chinese Women's Volleyball Team will endure

There are only ten days left in 2019. Today, I am making a 2020 training schedule in preparation of the Olympic Games.

Making a schedule for the next year has become part of my routine work since I began coaching the Chinese women's volleyball team eight years ago. However, my workload has been significantly reduced compared with the first two years.

I was determined to devote myself to this team when I became their head coach for the second time at the age of 53.

The sustainable development of a career needs the devotion of many people from generation to generation.

More than 40 years ago when the Chinese women's volleyball team started from scratch, my coach Yuan Weimin laid the foundation for their following development. Players of previous generations, including me, had been trying to turn impossibilities into realities under his guidance.

From then on, all coaches and players of the team have spared no efforts to make contributions to their development.

In 2013, I was still working in the volleyball circle when the team encountered new challenges on their way towards further progress. As a member of the older generation of the Chinese women's volleyball team, I thought that I had a responsibility to do more for the team.

As I regarded my decision to become the head coach of the team as a new attempt, I neither cared whether this decision will lead to success nor hesitated for fear of failure.

The Chinese women's volleyball team have been developing in the right direction since they had been among the world's leading teams for many years. However, with the rapid advances in science and technology, people were gaining deeper insights. As a result, modern volleyball is undergoing profound changes, and the new challenges for our team are to keep a balance between tradition and innovation in the new era.

The key competitive advantage of the Chinese women's volleyball team lies in their high flexibility and agility based on their comprehensive competence. Nevertheless, in today's volleyball competitions, reliance on six or seven key players can no longer ensure long-term success as before. All coaches and athletes have to break out of their comfort zones to make new attempts.

During our exploration, we can draw on the experiences

accumulated by our predecessors. However, we also need to be bold enough to forge ahead regardless of the difficulties and challenges.

Throughout the seven or eight years, very few could adhere to our cause from the very beginning to the end. Many people joined us but quit halfway. I may have forgotten some details without the reminder by this book that records our growth. However, I can still vividly remember the facial expressions of these players when they joined the team, and the regret and reluctance of those who had to part from us out of different reasons.

Along the way, we have been constantly improving ourselves by admitting our faults and making timely adjustments accordingly. We have been aiming to keep the Chinese women's volleyball team to remain dynamic and make more progress. As long as every effort is made towards this direction, we can gain peace of mind.

I will always remember what Coach Yuan said, "The head coach of the Chinese women's volleyball team must be both selfless and fearless."

In fact, the secret of the unique spirit of the Chinese women's volleyball team lies in the fact that it never gives up in spite of whatever difficulties and hardships. Instead of winning the championship every time, what really matters for the team is that it is always ambitious for winning the championship.

The Chinese team have been maintaining self-reliance

and self-improvement when they are at a low ebb and staying true to their commitment in their prime.

"The Challenges and Glory: The Journey of the Chinese Women's Volleyball Team" records the growth of our national team.

I appreciate this true record.

Though we will get old, the spirit of the Chinese women's volleyball team will endure.

Lang Ping

December 20, 2019

CONTENTS

INTRODUCTION

Ten consecutive victories!

On September 28, 2019, the penultimate round of the FIVB Volleyball Women's World Cup saw the competition between China and Serbia that ranked first in the world. When it was 24-16 in the third set, the two words "championship point" were shown clearly on the large screen.

The Chinese fans who came to Osaka, Japan to cheer for the Chinese women's volleyball team, were bursting into thunderous cheers with hundreds of overseas Chinese in Japan and the Chinese journalists in the stadium. They waved five-star red flags and shouted "China! China!"

In their presence, Lang Ping and her team won one more world championship.

This moment seemed both familiar and strange.

On September 2, 2015, in Nagoya, Japan, the Chinese women's volleyball team competed for the world champion after a lapse of 11 years.

In the final round the young Chinese team competed with the host Japan.

When the "championship point" came, Lang Ping brought on Wei Qiuyue as substitute, who had been struggling for one year against her injuries and finally returned to the court. Lang hoped this would allow Wei, a veteran who had gone through hardships, to experience the moment of glory on the court.

With a hard spike by Zhu Ting, the Chinese women's volleyball team won the world championship!

So many Chinese fans, with tears in their eyes, saw the members of the Chinese team standing on the world champion's podium.

Three years ago, the Chinese women's volleyball team got off to a bad start at the 2016 Rio Olympic Games, ultimately pushing themselves to the unfavorable condition of having to compete with the host Brazil for a top-four seat.

Given the fact that the Chinese team had lost 18 matches in a row to Brazil over the previous eight years, outplaying Brazil was almost impossible for the Chinese team.

"As the Chinese team are featured by the unyielding spirit, we will never give up! Though we are not on our 'home turf', we are supported by hundreds of millions of Chinese!" said Lang Ping before the match.

China lost the first set 15-25 and was under overwhelming pressure from Brazil during the second set. While the competition was intensified, the Chinese girls played to their enormous potential and turned the situation around!

The two teams came to the deciding set. Again, it was Zhu Ting who helped the Chinese team win the match point!

It was her back-row spike that not only took down hotly-tipped Brazil but also fully demonstrated the confidence and strength of the Chinese players!

The Chinese women's volleyball team advanced into the semifinal and was preparing for the ultimate championship.

In 2018, in the semifinals of the FIVB Volleyball Women's World Championship in Yokohama, Japan, the Chinese women's volleyball team, while still experiencing reshuffle, met Italy, one of the top teams.

After going five, the Chinese team lost by two points in

this tough match.

At that moment many fans who had been looking forward to Lang Ping's leading her team to win the "triple crown" could not help crying. They had the unshakable premonition that this might be the last world championship for the 57-year-old Lang Ping.

However, Lang Ping, still with a smile, encouraged her players: "The match is not over yet. Let's keep trying! Though there is no chance to play our national anthem, we must try our best to have our five-starred red flag raised during the awarding ceremony!"

Inspired by Lang Ping's words, the girls wiped their tears and returned to the court. They made great efforts to outplay the Netherlands, the last opponent, 3-0. Their performance showed that, instead of just for winning the championship, the spirit of the Chinese team fully embodied their perseverance despite the fact they had no chance to win.

On September 29, 2019, they won again!

It was the 10th world champion title for this heroic team over the past 39 years since the team won their first world champion title in 1981, and the third time that Lang and her team climbed to the top of the podium.

From 2013 when she began coaching the Chinese team for the second time, Lang Ping led the team to win the world championship for three times after addressing many challenges.

And all their stories began here.

CHAPTER ONE

2013

Do not go too far to forget why you started

In 2013 when the cycle of preparing for the Rio Olympic Games began, the Chinese team for the Games still had not been established.

The much-delayed appointment of the head coach reflected the low morale across the Chinese volleyball community.

At the 2012 London Olympic Games, the Chinese team lost to their longtime opponent Japanese team after going five in the quarterfinals. In the subsequent Asian Cup, China was upset by Thailand again.

Given the fact that the Chinese team had lagged behind their counterparts of Japan, South Korea and Thailand in Asia and relegated themselves to be among the second-class teams in the world, no one had much expectation for their performance at the 2016 Rio Olympic Games three and a half years later.

At that time, with her five-year coaching contract with Guangdong Evergrande Women's Volleyball Club drawing to a close, Lang Ping began to look forward to her leisure life after retirement. Though Lang Ping still wanted to contribute more to China's volleyball cause, she also had realized that people of her age should no longer work as hard as before.

After experiencing failure at the 2012 London Olympic Games, Xu Yunli, Wei Qiuyue and other senior players were still at a loss, wondering when and how they should phase out. However, they never gave up their stubborn and unwilling ambition regardless of their idea of retirement.

Before young players like Hui Ruoqi and Zeng Chunlei, who were in their heyday, began their preparation for new matches, what they were most concerned about was who would be the head coach to lead them forward in the following four years.

At that time, Zhu Ting, who had not fully recovered from malnutrition, and Zhang Changning, who was not sure about her future development, were both preparing in their respective teams for the youth-group competition of the National Games of China. It was nearly half a year ago the 16-year-old Yuan Xinyue became the MVP of the FIVB Volleyball Girls' U18 World Championship. Gong Xiangyu was still an ordinary junior setter, and Li Yingying of the millennial generation just graduated from primary school. None of them rose to fame then.

Winter jasmine blossomed after a sandstorm hit Beijing in the spring.

It was of great urgency to decide the head coach of the Chinese women's volleyball team.

1.

Was it possible that Lang Ping would take the post?

Lang Ping, who was known as the "Iron Hammer", came under the spotlight of the public when the Chinese team were in trouble again.

Lang Ping joined the Chinese team at 18 and took the lead in winning China's first championship of three major ball matches at 21, namely volleyball, basketball and soccer. As one of the important participants of the Chinese team that "claimed five successive world championships", she is an iconic figure of the Chinese team.

In 1986, Lang Ping, after announcing her retirement, went to the United States for further study despite numerous injuries resulting from her athlete career. For the past 27 years, whenever the Chinese team got into trouble, people concerned always hoped that Lang Ping would offer a helping hand.

There was no exception this time.

A year ago, at the 2012 London Olympic Games, China was upset by Japan, their longtime opponent. Lang Ping happened to be the commentator for this match at the invitation of CCTV, and she couldn't help shedding tears on the screen. The public in China was deeply moved by her genuine love towards the Chinese team.

On the morning of March 27th, when preparing Guangdong Evergrande Women's Volleyball Club for the matches of the Asian Women's Volleyball Club Championship, Lang Ping received an unfamiliar phone call. It turned out to be from the newly appointed director of the China Volleyball Management Center, who invited her back to Beijing for an interview.

Instinctively, Lang Ping declined the offer to serve again as the head coach of the Chinese team.

Unexpectedly, just after declining politely the invitation by the director, Lang Ping learned from a sudden call from her long-term teammate Zhang Rongfang that their teammate Chen Zhaodi had passed away, which was a really bad news for Lang.

Lang Ping sank in the sofa and failed to get up all afternoon. She kept weeping while recalling the past.

Lang Ping and Chen Zhaodi met in 1979.

In 1981 when the Chinese team won their first world championship, they were roommates. On the night of China's winning the championship, it was Lang Ping that carried Chen Zhaodi, who had injured her waist, back to their room.

Chen Zhaodi was really a workaholic in the Chinese team and nicknamed "one-armed general" because she once competed on the court even with her injured left arm bandaged. The waist injury of Chen Zhaodi was so serious that she was carried off the court by her teammates. This was the fifth similar case in her 11-year volleyball career.

Back to the room, Chen Zhaodi could do nothing but lay at full length in bed. Lang Ping helped her take baths, washed her clothes, and packed her luggage…

After learning the death of Chen Zhaodi, Lang Ping started to re-examine the offer to invite her to serve as the head coach of the Chinese team. She realized that this might be the last chance for her to pass on the valuable spirit of the women's volleyball team of her generation to the younger generations.

Realizing that she was willing to accept this offer, Lang Ping really admired her own courage.

She quite understood the heavy burden for the head coach of the Chinese team because she once assumed this post at the age of 34. The pressure, responsibility and workload involved were so overwhelming that she couldn't help feeling a headache whenever she recalled them. At that time, though still at a youthful age, she fainted on the court twice because of overwork. She didn't tell her parents about this. Later, when Lang's parents learned it in the newspaper, they were so inconsolable that tears came to their eyes.

"This time even if I want to take the post, my mother will certainly disagree!" Lang Ping said to herself.

On Sunday, when the team were off, she asked her mother and sister to dine out and wanted to take this chance to know their attitudes. Unexpectedly, when she just began, her mother and sister almost figured out what was on her mind. They reacted straightforwardly exactly as what they did over ten years ago: "You just focus on doing it and we will take care of the family!"

Lang Ping thought of her daughter again.

The last time when she became the head coach of the Chinese team, her daughter Bai Lang was only two years old. As Lang Ping packed up and drove away from home, she was so heartbreaking that she couldn't look back. Later, when Bai Lang was growing up, her biggest wish was that her mother was working at the McDonald's restaurant near her home.

Seventeen years later, the little girl who sat on her mother's lap at the medal award ceremony of the 1996 Atlanta

Olympic Games grew up and was about to graduate from the university. Lang Ping did not expect that her daughter had also deeply felt her profound love towards volleyball and the Chinese team. "Mother, you are still young. You should do whatever you want," said her daughter.

However, Lang Ping was still very hesitant. She couldn't retreat once she made the choice. She was not sure whether she could shoulder the responsibility both physically and psychologically. However, at the very thought that her achievements should be attributed to the efforts by the Chinese team, she felt duty-bound to help this team despite any challenge.

With only three and a half years left before the 2016 Rio Olympic Games, neither assistant coach nor a well-established team were available yet. The team consisted of both veteran and inexperienced players. Even worse, they didn't have a good command of the required technical skills. The time was too limited for Lang Ping to comprehensively improve their proficiency.

In 1995, it was the invitation by Yuan Weimin repeatedly, her respected mentor, that helped her determine to take the post. She still remembered what Yuan said then: "Lang Ping, the national team really needs you."

In order to live up to her mission, Lang Ping, though not quite experienced in coaching then, made every effort to lead the Chinese team back to the champion of Asia and went on to win silver medals of the Olympic Games and the FIVB Volleyball Women's World Championship. At the end of 1998, with tears in her eyes, she handed over a volleyball, the symbol of the Chinese team, to her successor Hu Jin.

She never expected that 15 years later she would again stand at the crossroads that may decide the fate of the Chinese team.

On April 15, 2013, after hours of deliberation during the previous night, Lang Ping appeared at the competition conference for the head coach in preparation for the participation of the Chinese team in the 2016 Rio Olympic Games. At the conference, she submitted her well-planned four-year schedule.

According to her plan, it would take one year to determine the 18 members of the national team, in which the veteran players could share their experiences with the younger ones, and train promising young players in preparation for the next Olympic Games. It aimed to secure the leading position of the Chinese team in Asia by the end of 2014. It aimed to upgrade the Chinese team from a second-class team to one of the world's leading teams by 2015. It aimed to make a breakthrough in the competition of the 2016 Rio Olympic Games.

On April 25, 2013, Lang Ping began coaching the Chinese team for the second time, which attracted wide attention. (Photo by Li Zhiyan)

2.

After serving as the head coach of the Chinese team, Lang Ping immediately asked every player to fill in a questionnaire including many questions as follows:

What are your characteristics? What are your technical features? What in your opinion is the goal of the national team in the Rio Olympic Games? What can you contribute to the team? Please list whatever additional help you expect from your coach.

Upon their first day of reporting to the national team, the players were assigned the questionnaire by Hu Jin, the team manager. Lang Ping was still in Vietnam at that time. She had to lead the Evergrande Women's Volleyball Team to complete their competitions in the Asian Women's Volleyball Club Championship before officially taking over the Chinese team.

The Chinese players could hardly finish the questionnaire at one go because they had to spend time on deliberation and organizing language. They found it really a good way to communicate with themselves before meeting the new goal. They also regarded it as their first-time communication with the well-known Coach Lang.

After returning to Beijing from the Asian Women's Volleyball Club Championship, Lang Ping packed up and moved into the Athlete Apartments of the Temple of Heaven at the same night. On their way to the apartments, while driving the car, her elder sister repeatedly reminded her to take good care of her health while working hard.

Lang Ping agreed with her sister. However, she knew it

was not up to her. She had to spare no efforts when required.

Hu Jin had put the completed questionnaires on Lang Ping's desk. She flipped through them and would pay special attention to the names of the players whose handwriting was graceful. Because the Chinese players of the older generation grew up in the era in which personal feelings were expressed via letters, they always felt as if they really saw their friends when reading letters from them.

Sitting at her desk, Lang Ping began reading the questionnaires. She wanted to finish all of them before meeting the girls the next day.

On May 10, 2013, the first day Lang Ping officially began leading the team, she arrived 15 minutes earlier than the scheduled training time for the team.

From 18 to 26, and from 34 to 38, she spent her best years on the national team. Lang Ping, then at the age of 53, was back.

When she entered the training hall, the lights inside were all on and the staff were still cleaning up the hall.

Lang Ping changed into her training clothes and sneakers. Seeing that the players had not arrived yet, she took out a notebook from her bag and wrote down a few words under the training schedule. Moments later, the Chinese players arrived by bus and walked into the hall one by one, each with earphones and being immersed in their respective rhythms.

Xu Yunli, Yang Junjing, Zeng Chunlei, Wang Yimei, Hui Ruoqi and Zhang Xian were all "senior team members" who had experienced the preparation cycle of the 2012 London Olympic Games. Seeing Lang Ping working, they dared not disturb her and walked straight into the hall.

The setter Shen Jingsi saw Lang Ping with a casual glance when going to the storage room to get something. When Shen was a little surprised, Lang Ping raised her head: "Xiaokui, run forward!" Shen was so surprised as she never expected that Coach Lang knew her nickname.

When the team members almost got ready, Lang Ping stood up and said loudly, "Gather together." The girls rushed over and formed two lines according to height.

The photographer rushed to take a group photo, which recorded the 22 people who participated in the first-phase training camp in 2013, including 14 athletes, 6 coaches and 2 medical doctors.

Lang Ping did not prepare any special opening remarks. Instead, she went straight to the point and immediately announced her morning training schedule.

3.

Lang Ping was observing the team members after the warm-up exercises began. When seeing any player failing to meet the requirements, Lang would go to remind the player and timely help her make corrections.

Over the years, when leading the overseas professional clubs, the U.S. National team or Guangdong Evergrande Women's Volleyball Club, she always started with helping the players correct mistakes and get rid of their bad habits. She always emphasized that the more one practices wrong playing actions, the farther one is away from goal.

After the warm-up exercises, Bao Zhuang, and Yuan Lingxi, the two trainers were ready to go on the court when

Lang Ping asked them to give her the ball. In the first round, she wanted to spike the ball herself.

"Try not to fall down when defending! Try to keep your balance! Remember to move your feet first!"

Lang Ping's voice was mixed with the shouting of the players, the continuous hitting of volleyballs, and the frequent squeak of sneakers when rubbing against the floor rubber.

After a class, Lang Ping's voice was mute.

Considering that the long-term training just began, the assistant coach Li Tieming wanted to buy a wireless microphone. Lang Ping didn't agree after thinking for a moment: "I'll be fine after I get used to it."

After two days of training, the assistant coach Lai Yawen asked Lang Ping, "We will set off next week, but there are only a few days left. Will we be off this Sunday?"

Lang Ping knew her concern. After Lang Ping became the head coach of the Chinese team, the public had much higher expectation for the team. However, in fact the new national team were just set up, the gap between them and their foreign counterparts could hardly be bridged within so short period of time. The new Chinese team were scheduled to attend competitions only after a few days of training. This would be a great challenge for the Chinese team because the opponents would include the Thailand team by which they were once defeated during the preparation cycle of the previous Olympic Games. The Chinese team were likely to be criticized if they lost again.

Lang Ping insisted on allowing the players to be off on Sunday. Pointing to her head, she said: "They can't absorb too much here. Let's go on next week."

In fact, on Sunday Lang Ping did not have to get up early as usual. However, she woke up incredibly early. Lying in bed, she was thinking about how to solve the problems identified during the training.

When Lang got up and picked up her mobile phone, she saw a message from her daughter from the United States and suddenly remembered that it was Mother's Day. She got up quickly and went to the living room, where she saw her 80-year-old mother making breakfast with her sister.

Seeing that the table was laid out with her favorite food, Lang Ping felt somewhat guilty: for so many years, whatever choice she makes, the whole family is fully supportive and does a good job of backing her up. Lang Ping had said over and over again that she would spend more time with her family after retirement one year later. However, it turned out that they had to go on supporting her on her job.

Lang Ping wanted to dine out to celebrate the Mother's Day. Her mother wanted her to have more rest at home. Therefore, she suggested they have lunch at home. This was exactly what Lang Ping wanted. It would allow her to chat with her mother at noon and return to her apartment early in the afternoon to review the players' training log. She wanted to reply to each player.

4.

Monday, May 13th. It was the fourth day after the Chinese team were established and the last day of the training camp in Beijing before the 4-nation women's volleyball invitational tournament.

Soon after the training started, the young setter Yao Di

was injured while making a defending action. Lang Ping asked other players to help Yao to the courtside and assisted her in applying ice packs to the injury.

When she saw the tears on Yao Di's face, Lang Ping touched her head and winked at her mischievously: "Di, are you tired of practicing and want to have a rest? The next time you want to take a break, you can tell me directly, I will give you a vacation. How painful it is to sprain your ankle!"

Experiencing Lang Ping's unique style of humor and optimism for the first time, Yao Di immediately relaxed and explained in Tianjin-style Mandarin: "Coach Lang, it's not like this."

During the break, Lang Ping walked to Yao, asking her why she sprained her ankle and whether she had any routine practices for enhancing her ankle strength. Yao Di shook her head and said, "I always wear ankle guards during training and matches."

Back in her seat, Lang whispered to Li Tieming, a coach in charge of physical training: "You should also pay more attention to the strength training of small joints. Wearing ankle guards doesn't always work."

Given the fact that the Chinese team had to improve their teamwork and prepare for the matches within less than one week before the competitions, Lang Ping followed the strategy of simplifying complicated problems and put all drills of basic skills and tactics into real practice, so as to focus on solving key problems.

The method of putting all technical details into real practice did work. The players kept making progress at a "visible" pace every day.

With minor adjustment to her team, Lang Ping led the

new Chinese team to outplay the Thailand team twice, which won wide acclaim. The Chinese team led by Lang Ping, the "Iron Hammer", attracted the attention of the women's volleyball fans of several generations. The Shenzhen Universiade Center Gymnasium set a record when it hosted a volleyball match for the first time. There were no empty seats in this 18000-seat gymnasium then.

The return of Lang Ping brought hope to many people who loved the Chinese team. But Lang Ping pleaded with the enthusiastic media: "Don't call the Chinese team as the Lang's Army."

5.

Back to Beijing from Shenzhen, Lang Ping "disappeared" with the team from the public for a few days.

The 27 days from May 27 to June 22 was the only period in 2013 for Chinese team to focus on training without interruption.

During these days, the Chinese players got up at 7 o'clock every morning, went to the training hall after breakfast and started training from 8:30 a.m. to 1:00 p.m. The training schedule was so tight that they could hardly have time for rest. After the nap up, there were physical training sessions in the afternoon, and then therapy sessions and video learning in the evening, etc. The schedule was pretty tight. The girls were off only in Thursday morning and on Sunday.

A week after the training began, Chen Zhan, a libero from Jiangsu province, suddenly received a transfer order from the national team. This was really good news she had been dreaming of. Feeling both excited and uneasy, she

The training schedule was very tight. Lang Ping and the Chinese players got up at 7 a.m. Their daytime training was followed by the therapy sessions and video learning in the evening. (Photo by Yin Di)

reported to the national team in Beijing. After a few days of training with the team, Chen Zhan was so tired that she even didn't want to talk.

Because Yan Ni gave up a ball that should not be missed in the training, Lang Ping imposed a penalty on her by ordering her to practice a set of "individual defence training".

During the practices, Yan Ni had to defend by herself half of the court.

Lang Ping was standing in the middle before the net. Bao Zhuang and Yuan Lingxi, the two male coaches, were facing towards Yan Ni from left to right, each with a basket of volleyballs behind them. All these balls would be served towards Yan Ni at high speed. Two other players, with towels in their hands, were ready to rush into the court to wipe clean the sweat left by Yan Ni when she fell. Others cheered on Yan Ni outside the court.

Upon the order of "20 good defence, start" by Lang Ping, the two male coaches alternated hard spikes with dink spikes, forcing Yan Ni to move around the court. There were both quantity and quality requirements for the balls defended by Yan Ni. Lang Ping had the final say on whether they were qualified or not.

The first few balls were fine for Yan Ni. However, with the increase in difficulty and the decline in her physical strength, Yan Ni, with a height of over 1.9 m, could hardly run anymore. Every time she tried her best to sprawl for saving the ball, traces of sweat would be found on the court here and there.

For a sprawl, Yan Ni fell heavily on the ground. Amid the cheering of Yan's teammates, Lang Ping began to count down, 10, 9, 8, 7... If Yan Ni failed to stand up before the countdown ended, one point will be deducted from the completed points.

Tears began to appear in Yan Ni's eyes. The male coach was ready to spike. Shouting out Yan Ni's name, other players encouraged her to stand up as soon as possible. As if using her last strength, Yan finally struggled to stand up and prepared for the next ball.

After finally finishing twenty times of qualified defence, Yan Ni, panting and crying, was helped off the court by her teammates.

At this moment, Lang Ping, who was usually humorous and considerate to the girls, put on a stern face. She once said: "The opponent will never compromise with you in the competition. Some hurdles must be cleared by yourself."

Compared with her efforts made in bridging the gap of technical skills, Lang Pin focused more on improving her team members' attitude and style of training.

Wang Yimei, a tall and strong player, was most afraid of the practice of supporting body with fingers. When it came to the finger-support session, she would try to hide out of Lang Ping's sight.

"Wang Yimei, where can you hide?" Lang Ping said jokingly when chasing after Wang Yimei.

Wang Yimei, with reluctance or hesitation, drew close to her teammates. Lang Ping pointed to the open space in front of her: "Come here, let me watch you do this!"

Lang Ping placed particular emphasis on practicing pushing-up with fingers. Previously, the Chinese players didn't spend enough time on practicing supporting body with fingers, so their fingers weren't strong enough. This resulted in their ineffective blocking and vulnerability to injury.

Plagued by injuries, Lang Ping often had to find somewhere to lean on for relieving pain during training. (Photo by Yin Di)

At the beginning of their drills, even these players who were light in weight could hardly do it. This was particularly difficult for Wang Yimei who was heavier in weight.

With each set of drill lasting for 40 seconds, Lang Ping used stopwatch to calculate time while overseeing the playing actions of the players. The body must be kept in a straight line, and must be supported with fingers, otherwise the time for practice must be extended. Each time Lang Ping called a halt, all Chinese players, especially Wang Yimei, grinned in pain. She checked her fingers so carefully as if she were afraid that one of them had been broken.

After the daytime training, Lang Ping would ask players to watch by video their respective performance in the matches after dinner.

Before the last training session of the training camp ended, Lang Ping called the players together and shared with them her expectation.

As the head coach, Lang Ping always had to replace old players with younger ones and the inferior ones with the superior ones. She knew that some players might never come back again after leaving the team. However, she hoped that as long as one had been once a member of the national team, the training experienced here would inspire her and lead to certain positive changes.

"Tomorrow we will start to prepare for the National Games. I hope you can apply what you have learned from practice to the competitions. Also, when you come back to your provincial team, you should share them with your teammates. On the court, in times of difficulty, any national team member should play a key role and take the initiative to assume responsibility in her provincial team. I hope you can bring back your high morale and technical skills to your provincial teams."

After seeing off the players that attended the first-phase training, Lang Ping began considering the name list of the second-phase training camp after the National Games.

6.

After returning from the National Games, Shen Jingsi found that she had a new roommate.

Zhu Ting, five years younger than her, was from Henan province. At first glance, she felt that "Zhu's legs are so long that it seems they start right down from her chest".

Lang Ping had instructed her to take care of Zhu Ting: "Do take good care of her. Take her out with you on weekends. Don't leave her alone in the room."

In fact, then Lang Ping knew little about Zhu Ting. Three years ago, in the China Women Volleyball League, a young girl with excellent jumping ability and coordinated movements from Henan province caught the attention of Lang Ping. Afterwards, Zhu Ting joined Guangdong Evergrande Women's Volleyball Club from Henan provincial volleyball team. When Lang Ping asked about the "girl with outstanding jumping ability", she learned from Wang Ting that the girl was named Zhu Ting. Born to a farmer's family in Zhoukou, Henan province, Zhu Ting was the third of five daughters in the family.

When selecting players for the new Chinese team, Coach Lang remembered Zhu Ting and wanted to give this girl a chance. When finding Zhu Ting was included in the name list of the national team, many people wondered who Zhu Ting was.

In fact, even Zhu Ting herself couldn't answer this question.

If Zhu Ting hadn't played volleyball, she might have become a migrant worker in a southern city with her two older sisters.

In 2007, Zhu Ting, a middle school student, was already close to 1.8 meters in height. The teacher in charge of her class suggested that she focus on developing her potential in sports because she was not among the most promising candidates vying for local key high schools. She first took part in the interview at the basketball team of Zhoukou Sports School. However, she was rejected because the coach complained that she was too thin. Then she went to the canoeing team for an interview, but was rejected again because her legs were too long to give full play to her strength on the canoe. Luckily, she was finally accepted by the coach of the volleyball team.

During the earliest days of her playing volleyball, Zhu Ting was so thin that she was most afraid of practicing sprawling to save the ball. After falling down on the wooden floor again and again, she was black and blue all over her body. She couldn't help weeping each time when calling her parents during that period. Her mother, being softhearted, wanted her daughter back, but her father always encouraged her to hold on to it.

"Fortunately, I had not enough money for a ticket back home, otherwise I would have gone home." After growing up, whenever recalling these hard days, Zhu Ting considered herself lucky enough not to have given up.

In 2008 when Henan Provincial Sports School selected outstanding juniors from the prefecture-level sports schools, Zhu Ting met the requirements of "height of over 1.8 m and under the age of 14". Therefore, she was selected to begin her professional volleyball training at the provincial team. A year later, she joined Henan Youth team of Volleyball. In 2010, at the age of sixteen, she played in the China Women Volleyball League on behalf of Henan team. In the match against Guangdong Evergrande Women's Volleyball Club, she met Lang Ping for the first time across the net.

In 2012, Zhu attended the Asian Youth Championships as a member of the National Youth Team and was awarded the Most Valuable Player (MVP) for the first time during her career.

In the spring of 2013, Zhu Ting, 18, was preparing as a member of Henan Youth Team for the youth competition of the National Games of the PRC.

When the name of Zhu Ting was found in the full name list of the national team that was just announced, her coach and teammates came to share the good news with Zhu Ting at the earliest time. She looked very composed, saying that she still needed to make more efforts for a few more years before becoming one of the key players.

"Except for my limited advantage in attacking ability, I was just a player of average level in the same age bracket. Also, my performance wasn't stable enough... I didn't know why all of a sudden, I played better than before during the Montreux Volley Masters, delivering remarkably stable performance throughout this match," recalled Zhu Ting.

As for the Montreux Volley Masters, the Chinese team usually sent their key players to take part in the event. However, in 2013, because both the appointment of the head coach and the formation of the national team were late than the schedule, and many matches were ahead in that year, Lang Ping decided not to dispatch the national team. Therefore, the Chinese Youth Team that would attend the 2013 FIVB Volleyball Women's U20 World Championship was sent for this event on behalf of China. Zhu Ting seized the opportunity by delivering quite good performance in the match.

Zhu Ting believed that nothing but sudden enlightenment could explain the unexpected magic change that happened to her, which helped her usher in her rocket-like rapid progress.

After rising to fame at the Montreux Volley Masters, Zhu Ting and her teammates of Chinese Youth Team won the 2013 FIVB Volleyball Women's U20 World Championship without losing one set throughout all the eight matches. She was awarded the titles of Best Scorer, Best Outside Spiker and Most Valuable Player. For the first time, the FIVB used "future superstar" to endorse her future potential.

On July 23, 2013, the first day Zhu Ting joined the training camp of the national team, she attracted wide attention.

With her bag on back and sneakers in hands, Zhu followed her roommate Shen Jingsi into the training hall. These senior players were talking and laughing as they changed their shoes and put on protective gear to prepare for the training. Zhu kept silent and only briefly responded when she was asked about.

Sitting on the floor during the warm-up exercises, Zhu looked shorter than her peers. "Her legs are so long," someone exclaimed. "Zhu Ting, how long are your legs?" Zhu Ting answered frankly: "Ah? I don't know. I haven't measured them."

Finally, when it was time for practicing spikes, everyone wanted to challenge Zhu Ting to check how tall she was. After several rallies, Zhang Xian, a libero, teased Ma Yunwen by saying, "In front of Xiao Zhu (Zhu Ting), whatever kind of jump you make will prove to be in vain, because your hands can't reach the same height as she does. Really, they're all super hands!" While all other players were bursting into laughter, Zhu Ting still remained quite calm.

A week later, Zhu traveled to Macau with the Chinese team for the first-week competitions of the World Women's Volleyball Grand Prix.

During the first set against Bulgaria, after scoring the first point for the Chinese team by a hard spike, Zhu Ting was so happy that she rushed for a victory lap for celebration, a symbolic posture of Zhu at the Chinese Youth League. She just ran half a lap before suddenly finding that her teammates were hugging each other in the central part of the court for her participation!

"Girl, we are too old to run. Don't forget to run back and hug us." Ma Yunwen's joking words amused Zhu Ting.

In this 3-0 victory, Zhu made her national team debut with an outstanding performance by scoring 18 points. This fully showed her outstanding gift and comprehension ability, thus securing her position as one of the key players of the national team.

As the Chinese team just began their preparation for the 2016 Rio Olympic Games, the return of Lang Ping and the outstanding performance of Zhu Ting were good news.

However, Lang Ping, was quite frank when mentioning Zhu Ting in her interview: "Zhu Ting is competent but still far from reaching her prime. What she has mastered can hardly ensure her long-term success in the international competitions."

It turned out that Lang Ping had planned a unique career progression for Zhu Ting who "resembles Lang of her youthful age in many ways", which was much more foresighted and future-oriented than expected by the public. Zhu Ting, despite her widely acknowledged natural gift, still had a long way to go before ultimately reaching the goal set by Lang Ping.

7.

From early spring to mid-summer, it only took the Chinese team four months to become a powerful team again after scoring victories in a row. The fans of the Chinese team didn't expect they could make so rapid progress.

At the World Women's Volleyball Grand Prix, from Macau to Hong Kong and then to Wuhan, the Chinese team competed in three cities one after another and won all the nine matches, advancing as the first-place team of this round into the finals to be held in Sapporo, Japan. The Chinese team last won the championship of this event in 2005.

What was even more impressive was the great art displayed by Lang Ping in deploying her team members.

In the competitions held in the three cities, 21 of the 22 Chinese players were given the chance to play on the court. Shen Jingsi, the chief setter, was the only one among the starting lineup of all matches. However, no one played throughout all the matches.

All of a sudden, the Chinese team were capable of competing against the world's top teams even with constant substitution for reserving players' physical strength. While marveling at Lang Ping's magic power, fans even had higher expectations for this team.

As soon as they arrived in Sapporo, Lang Ping held a meeting to ask her team members what their target of this event was.

All team members remained silent and waited for the instruction from Lang Ping. To their surprise, she said that it was acceptable if the Chinese team wouldn't be at the bottom.

Such a sharp contrast had started the girls all off laughing. However, Lang took it seriously:

"The previous glory such as Olympic champions and world champions belonged to the Chinese team of the elderly generation, rather than your generation. We, though a young team, need to have strong ambition to surpass our predecessors. However, we must be well positioned at first. Currently we shall not just focus on the results of each competition."

The girls nodded, but in fact they didn't fully understand what Lang meant.

In the first four match days before the finals began, China won Serbia, Italy, the United States and Japan in a row. They had nineteen straight wins after Lang Ping served as their head coach. The Chinese team led by Lang seemed overwhelmingly powerful.

In the final round, the Chinese team would compete against the Olympic champion Brazil. Which team would win at last, China or Brazil?

All the Chinese fans believed that it was a good opportunity, hoping that the Chinese team led by Coach Lang would win the Grand Prix by outplaying Brazil.

At that time, the Chinese team had lost twelve consecutive matches to Brazil within five years. During this period, after their 3-2 victory over Brazil in Beilun Grand Prix before the 2008 Beijing Olympic Games, China didn't defeat Brazil again. Even worse, the Chinese team even didn't win a set in seven matches.

Now, with Lang Ping as the head coach and the super

volleyball player Zhu Ting, the Chinese team had registered their 19th win in a row. It seemed that the Chinese team were powerful enough to compete against their Brazilian counterpart.

Unexpectedly, on the eve of the match, Lang Ping made a surprising decision: She would replace those key players including Zhu Ting, Hui Ruoqi and Xu Yunli with a new lineup.

When the Chinese team's lineup was unveiled the next day before the match, the public opinion was in an uproar, blaming Lang Ping for giving up such a good opportunity and wondering if she wanted to find excuse for losing the match.

As expected, the Chinese team, without these key players, were no match for their Brazilian counterpart. Brazil, the Olympic champion, continued their five-year victory over China by winning three sets in a row. However, it seemed that the shrewd Brazilian coach Jose Roberto Lages Guimaraes wasn't as excited as expected after their victory.

In response to the questioning by the media, Lang Ping replied: "Given their current capability and the consumption of physical strength after so many matches, the Chinese team were unlikely to win this match even if they tried their best."

Though no one retorted upon her publicly, the majority couldn't accept the fact that the Chinese team didn't try their best in this match.

She added that winning the champion wasn't the ultimate goal of the Chinese team as they still had a long way to go.

However, Lang Ping smiled but made no comment on how to meet the target and why the Chinese team didn't vie for every possible champion.

She was asked if it was a pity that the nineteen straight wins came to an end like this. She replied that such kind of wins were not really as important as they seemed. What if China met Brazil earlier?

After this match in the afternoon, there were still three hours before the award ceremony to be held in the evening. Therefore, the Chinese players were allowed to take time off. They could go out for a stroll, sample the local cuisine or just relax themselves.

When they parted at the gate of the hotel, Lang Ping said, "Don't forget to attend the award ceremony."

When the girls assured her in chorus, she teased them in a humorous way: "Of course, you can be late if you don't want to receive the award..."

Amid the laughter, the Chinese girls dispersed quickly to go shopping in the streets of Sapporo.

8.

From Sapporo to Beijing and then to Bangkok, the Chinese team won the runner-up of the World Women's Volleyball Grand Prix. This team were likely to embrace a satisfactory result in 2013.

During the three-hour drive from Bangkok's Suvarnabhumi International Airport to Khorat, Lang Ping wanted to have a rest, but something was always on her mind.

It was her 127th day after she took charge of the Chinese team again.

From their 19 wins in a row, it seemed that the Chinese

team became more competitive. In fact, however, it should be attributed to the players' higher spirit and morale. From the technical and tactical perspectives, it was Lang Ping's experience that helped the team give full play to their potential and minimize their faults. In essence, the team hadn't made significant progress in terms of their strength. Instead, they still had many disadvantages to be identified.

The Asian Women's Volleyball Championship was the only real challenge for the Chinese team that year. Lang Ping chose the twelve players who were in the best shape. However, she was still not quite sure about her choice, because her players were subject to emotional instability under pressure, which might hamper their performance. If so, the Chinese team would be put at a great disadvantage in the competitions.

The first goal set by Lang Ping after she became the head coach was to regain the leading position in Asia by winning the Asian championship again. First, she led the team to make a thorough study of the Thailand team, the host country team of the Asian Women's Volleyball Championship.

Although relatively short in stature, the players of Thailand had superior physical strength. They had been playing volleyball together for years, featuring various tactical combinations, playing approaches and unique cooperation. However, over the previous several years, the Chinese team failed to pay enough attention to the training of basic skills. As a result, they were always at a disadvantage in the competitions with Thailand team. The Chinese players could hardly hold on for several rallies because they found it difficult to keep up with Thailand team's fast speed and organize effective defence against the opponent's attack.

On September 20, Thailand's local time, China and Thailand met in the semifinals.

It happened to be Friday. All seats were occupied in the 4,000-capacity Chatchai Hall long before the match started. As soon as the two teams appeared, the deafening sound of gongs and drums, combined with the cheering of the fans, was so strong that it almost broke through the stadium ceiling.

It was the first time for Zhu Ting to see such a challenge posed by the advantage of the opponent's home turf. This reminded her of what Lang Ping emphasized at the preparation meeting. Lang said to them, "You need to prepare for the trickiest situation. No matter how loudly the spectators shout, you must try your best to control yourself. Stay calm and clear-headed."

The well-prepared Chinese team got off to a good start, winning the first set 25-19. Competing on their home turf, the Thailand team tried to catch up and began to step up their efforts in the second set and delivered increasingly better performance amid the cheering of their compatriots. Under such intense pressure, the Chinese team made more mistakes, losing two sets 19-25 and 22-25 in a row.

With more fans present and the cheering becoming louder and louder, Lang Ping and the players had to shout to each other to make their voices heard. Their voices gradually became hoarse. Zhu Ting touched her face and ears frequently and murmured to herself, "Why are my face and ears so hot?"

In the fourth set, the Chinese players gritted their teeth and won the chance of playing for the deciding set.

The Thailand team took a 4-0 lead at the beginning of the deciding set. The frequent substitution of the Chinese team failed to reverse the unfavorable situation. The Thailand team seized two match points before the Chinese team tied the score up at 14-14 with Xu Yunli's quick attack and Shen

Jingsi's blocking. At the crucial moment, the Thailand team consecutively scored two points and won the match when a digging by a Chinese player failed under a direct spike by the opponent.

The match ended, and it was one more heartbroken failure, especially at a time when the Chinese team were on their way up and everyone had high expectation for them. In some ways, the players felt even more frustrated than a year ago.

From striving for the championship to competing for the third-place match, these Chinese girls could hardly accept such harsh reality and calm down within less than 24 hours.

The next day, when competing with the South Korea team that had also lost in the semifinals, the Chinese team lost again after winning the first two sets and then losing three ones in a row.

The Chinese team finished fourth in the Asian Women's Volleyball Championship. It was their worst ever performance during 38 years after they took part in the event in 1975.

No one had expected the result, and it was even harder to associate the worst ever performance with Lang Ping, a veteran coach who had led teams to so many victories. People wondered, from the runner-up in the FIVB World Grand Prix to the fourth place in the Asian Women's Volleyball Championship, whether the Chinese team led by Lang Ping stayed on the right track of catching up with the world's top teams or they had degraded to one of the second-class teams in Asia.

Lang Ping was exposed to the unprecedented crisis of confidence she ever met after she took office. Some people even called for her resignation.

Shen Jingsi, a setter to whom Lang Ping had given special

instructions over the previous year, couldn't help weeping. Still with tears in her eyes, she wrote a letter to Lang Ping. However, she didn't dare to knock on the door of Lang's room. After pondering for a moment, she slipped the letter under the door.

After the failure, Zhang Xian, the libero, sank into deep self-reproach. She, one of the veterans who had gone through the cycle of London Olympic Games, was eager to fight for the national team led by Lang Ping for four more years. Over the previous four months, she kept writing down technical tips according to the instructions of her coach and all the details and her feelings in her diary every day, because she really cherished the experience during this period. That night, she stood outside the door of Lang's room for half an hour and tried to say sorry to Lang.

After great deliberation, Xu Yunli decided to send Lang a message via WeChat. "Coach Lang, you have done so much for us. I am really sorry that we failed to live up to your expectations."

Lang replied via WeChat at once to her. "Since I chose to coach this team, I am ready for any challenges. This is just a beginning. I will try my best to work hard with everyone to fulfil our task every day. I do not expect anything in return. I only hope that we can work together to make continuous progress, during which mutual encouragement is needed, and I will try my best to be initiative-taking and achieve self-improvement."

Lang Ping encouraged herself to firmly pursue her predetermined target.

CHAPTER TWO

2014

Sixteen years have passed since Lang Ping resigned as the head coach of the Chinese national team

Before all the tasks of the Chinese team in 2013 were completed, Lang Ping held a nationwide initial audition of unprecedented scale at the end of October.

This event attracted the participation of Ding Xia, a young setter of the women's volleyball team of Liaoning province, the teammate of Zhu Ting in Chinese Youth Team, which won the 2013 FIVB Volleyball Women's U20 World Championship, and some volleyball players of the new generation who delivered outstanding performance in China's domestic league, etc. Most notably, Lang Ping also selected Yuan Xinyue, the middle blocker of Bayi Volleyball Team, who had recently won the MVP of the FIVB Volleyball Girls' U18 World Championship. The girl, only sixteen, stood at 1.99 meter.

Zhu Ting, whose height was about to exceed 1.95 meter, was happy to have a new teammate who was nearly two meters in height, and she was no longer the tallest and the most conspicuous player in the team.

The first few days of the audition even saw the participation of two young men—Yu Fei from Tianjin and Li Tong from Jiangsu province.

Lang Ping learned from the training and competitions over the previous year that the male trainers of the women's volleyball team also needed to be replaced with younger ones. To help improve the strength of the team, the male trainers must be young and vigorous enough and capable of executing both precise and powerful spikes.

During the breaks of training, Lang Ping walked out

of the training hall while speaking English on her mobile phone. She was contacting the top physical trainers, rehabilitation therapists and sports traumatology doctors in the United States, hoping they could arrive as expected before the training camp of the Chinese team began in 2014.

In the aftermath of the failure of the Chinese team in the Asian Women's Volleyball Championship, Lang Ping had forged ahead without hesitation when some were still wondering whether she was qualified for transforming the Chinese team or not. Despite all these unfavorable factors, Lang Ping emphasized that she had made determination after thorough deliberation during the 20 days in the spring of 2013. She said she wouldn't retreat once she made the decision.

1.

The 27-member list of the Chinese team in 2014 was unveiled after extensive trial training of 2013 and review of the performance of players during the national league and the statistics of athletic talents of appropriate age across China in 2013.

Only six members of the team that attended the 2012 London Olympic Games remained, including Xu Yunli and Wei Qiuyue, as well as Hui Ruoqi, Yang Junjing, Zeng Chunlei and Shan Danna who made rapid progress in the preparation cycle of the 2012 London Olympic Games. The reshuffle of the national team showed that Lang Ping was determined to recruit younger players to the national team.

More responsible young coaches were needed to identify and train more young players.

"Being the coach of the Chinese team requires my full devotion." Lang Ping recalled what her coach Yuan Weimin told her 20 years ago, when she saw the new coaches, including An Jiajie, Wu Xiaolei, Yu Fei and Li Tong, and the coaches who had worked in the team for many years, like Bao Zhuang and Yuan Lingxi.

The most significant change was the participation of foreign experts in the Chinese team for the first time.

Dr. Sherwin S. W., a renowned surgeon at Pritzker School of Medicine of the University of Chicago, worked with Lang Ping six years ago. He was a member of the U.S. Olympic Committee's Sports Medicine Commission, and once served as a medical doctor of the U.S. women's volleyball team coached by Lang Ping. Lang Ping called him "Doctor Ho".

She hoped that the Chinese players could benefit from the excellent expertise of Doctor Ho, who could alleviate their pain caused by injuries, and as a result their athletic career could be extended.

Elizabeth Darling, a physiotherapy Ph.D. with certificates of sports coach and specialist clinician in bone trauma, had 13-year work experience with a number of leading physical therapy and rehabilitation institutions, and had supplied specially appointed sports medical service to several U.S. Olympic teams. It was the sincere invitation by Lang Ping that finally persuaded this female rehabilitation therapist to leave her family and children for China alone to help the Chinese team better recover from injuries.

2.

It was cloudy and drizzly in Zhangzhou this April.

Lang Ping returned to Zhangzhou 16 years after resigning from the head coach of the Chinese team in 1998.

Zhangzhou had changed a lot after more than ten years. Out of the Zhangzhou Base, one couldn't tell the difference between other cities and Zhangzhou adorned with towering skyscrapers and flashing neon. The Tengfei Museum and the Three-peat Monument at the crossroad were no longer among the city's most prominent landmarks. However, the volleyball gym of Zhangzhou Base saw the great efforts made by several generations of the Chinese team here.

From her first visit to Zhangzhou for the training camp of the Chinese team in 1976 to her retirement from the Chinese team in 1986, each year Lang Ping and her teammates underwent the most arduous training in Zhangzhou.

After Lang Ping served as the head coach of the Chinese team in 1995, it was Zhangzhou that witnessed how they addressed the great challenges.

Learning that the Chinese team led by Lang Ping would return to Zhangzhou, the former director, the office staff and the clinic doctors of the Base all came back to visit Lang Ping. Once the key staff of the Base 20 or 30 years ago, they had been 70 or 80 years old then. However, the memory of each other was still their appearance of youthful age.

In December 1972, Zhangzhou held the first-phase national youth volleyball winter training camp. At that time, the training hall was made by bamboo shed. The ground was paved with tabia consisting of cinders below and lime and laterite above mixed by salt water. Since there was no dormitory, they had to live in the dormitory of a local Cadre School of Finance and Trade. Only well water was available. They could only take a bath once a day in a nearby factory. Even the physical training equipment such as barbell was brought by the team members from their own municipal and provincial teams.

Practicing on the ground made of tabia first needed the spirit of devotion. When one fell on the ground, his or her clothes would be scratched, shoes would be broken, and skin would be scraped, with grains of sand from the tabia ground embedded in the flesh, which caused immediate bleeding. After a day of training, the congeals of blood and the training suits would be stuck together. At night doctors had to separate them bit by bit with tweezers and pick out the small grains of sand embedded in the flesh. When they got up the next morning, the wounds on the athletes would be stuck to the sheets again, which required nurses to help rip open them bit by bit.

After forty-two years, when mentioning the "bamboo

shed spirit" that laid the foundation for the rise of the Chinese women's volleyball team, Gu Huaqun could still instinctively react with the following statement: Practicing solid skills and aspiring to reach the top in spite of any hardship or challenge.

Gu Huaqun, who was about of the same age as Lang Ping's parents, oversaw the Zhangzhou training camp when Lang Ping first went here in 1976. "Last time we met, you were thirty-eight and I was sixty-five. Now you are fifty-four and I am eighty-one. Time passed so quickly that the young girl then has become an elderly lady." Gu Huaqun smiled while patting Lang Ping on her shoulder.

3.

On April 29, after competing in the Asian Women's Volleyball Club Championship, Wei Qiuyue flew from Tianjin to Xiamen and then transferred to Zhangzhou.

She didn't find the courage to reflect on the previous year until she finally embarked on her new journey after going through many setbacks.

About one year ago, depressed by the failure in the 2012 London Olympic Games, Wei Qiuyue determined to retire. However, she at once changed her mind and determined to make a new start for another four years upon hearing the news that Lang Ping would become the head coach of the national team. When she made up her mind, she forgot her injured legs that were weaker than before. Having played in two Olympic Games, she wanted to seize this opportunity to make a breakthrough.

However, she did not find her name in the name list of

Wei Qiuyue, the captain of the Chinese team during the 2012 London Olympic Games, had planned to retire as the result of the Chinese team's failure during the Olympic Games. However, she at once changed her mind and determined to make a new start for another four years upon hearing the news that Lang Ping would become the head coach of the national team.
(Photo by Li Zhiyan)

the new national team. Plagued by her ardent desire and the cruel reality, she felt a sense of loss that she had never experienced before.

After hesitation for eight months, she finally screwed up her courage to send a short message to Lang Ping for the first time. It was also the first time that she directly expressed to Lang Ping her aspiration to play for the national team. Lang Ping's reply helped her regain the confidence to prove herself. In the following China Women Volleyball League, Wei Qiuyue delivered her performance in a "magical" manner. As a result, Tianjin Women's Volleyball Team were transformed miraculously under her leadership. At the weekend before the end of the League, while dining out with her friends, Wei Qiuyue received a call from Lang Ping.

"Coach Lang asked about my recent situation such as my recovery from the injuries and my future plan. I reported my injuries truthfully and told her in a very sincere and solemn manner that I was willing to make further contribution to the Chinese team. However, Coach Lang did not give me a straight answer. Instead, she said that this year an American rehabilitation therapist would join the training camp of the national team. She was confident in helping me keep my injuries under control."

A week later, Wei Qiuyue saw her name on the name list of national team's training camp.

After arriving at the gate of the national team apartment at the Zhangzhou Base with her suitcase, she stood there silently for several minutes before entering.

The last time she stood here was before the 2012 London Olympic Games when Xu Yunli, Wang Yimei, Ma Yunwen, Zhang Xian and she sat before the reception counter for a group photo. They all said they might not have a chance to come back.

A year and a half later, when Wei Qiuyue returned here, only Xu Yunli was here waiting for her.

Later, they made an agreement during a chat that this time they would try their best to make further contribution to the Chinese team not only for themselves, but also for their previous teammates who had no chance to come back.

4.

The team had three training sessions a day in Zhangzhou.

After the daytime training and dinner, Lang Ping went back to her room for a rest and then knocked on the door of Lai Yawen who was in the room across the aisle. She wanted, together with Lai, to urge Xu Yunli, Yang Junjing and several other players who were good at serving, to further fine-tune their serving skills by paying more attention to details.

Before the training in groups began, Lang Ping gathered all the players that attended the night training and told them, "There are no best but better skills. Especially we don't have a unique technical skill that we can boast. Now we should make full use of this period to hone our skills. We should start from standardizing our playing actions and try to make progress by improving details. The task today is to practice serving. We need to get the action right first, and then to focus on improving the attacking power, stability and accuracy of the serving."

An Jiajie, the assistant coach, oversaw the training of Zhu Ting and Yuan Xinyue.

Zhu soon found out her problems. She could perform standard actions without holding a ball, but was still unable to perform well when serving a ball. Instead of giving up, Zhu tried several times again but failed to achieve the expected results. To help her gain deeper insight into the nuances, Coach An shot a few videos with his mobile phone. Then they analyzed the root cause through slow-motion playback of the videos.

As for Yuan Xinyue, she progressed quite smoothly.

The united team of Chinese players during the break. They consisted of veteran ones: Wei Qiuyue (R4), Xu Yunli (R3), Hui Ruoqi (L3) and Yang Junjing (L4), and newbies including Zhu Ting (R2) and Ding Xia (L1). (Photo by Zeng Zhen)

Inspired by the instructions of Coach An, she suddenly understood how to control her arm at the moment of exerting her power. After making several floating serves of excellent rotation and landing points, Yuan Xinyue wanted to test the effectiveness via real practice. So, she ran to the libero Chen Zhan for help.

Xu Yunli and Yang Junjing worked so hard in serving balls that they began sweating heavily. However, they were still not quite satisfied with the quality and the landing point of service. Lai Yawen stood by to shoot videos to be used for analyzing the root cause and working out a solution. Then they tried again.

The coaches were quite glad to see the players were so self-motivated during the training.

Lai Yawen said jokingly, "Previously, it was the coach who

decided whether the action was qualified or not. Now it is up to the player herself. Please do keep such momentum!"

After two-hour night training, on their way back to the apartment, An Jiajie still gesticulated to show how to swing the arm when serving and Zhu Ting followed suit. She hoped that doing so would help her gain better feeling when resuming training the next day.

As they went upstairs, Lang Ping quietly reminded An Jiajie, "The players' basic skills are far from perfect. Since improvement of such skills needs long-term efforts, we shouldn't expect it to be achieved at one stroke. Otherwise, under the pressure, they might have no idea of what to do. So, we have to patiently explain it in details and give them enough time to understand it. There is still room for improvement for our players, including the veterans. We need to try to make them feel they are capable, which requires our special patience."

2014 was the second year after Zhu Ting joined the national team.

Before the training camp began, Lang Ping had a heart-to-heart talk with Zhu Ting. Lang said that Zhu needed to comprehensively improve her technical expertise if she wanted to become a better outside hitter. Lang expected her to achieve further self-improvement by having a firm target and calm mind.

Zhu Ting quite agreed with what Lang Ping said and thus made up her mind.

During the technical training course in this afternoon, Coach Bao Zhuang and Li Tong guided Zhu Ting, Liu Xiaotong and other outside hitters on practicing serve receiving. During the training of the previous day, Bao Zhuang stood next to Zhu Ting and counted the success rate of her serve receiving. She didn't play well. Her serve receiving always failed to reach the expected landing point. Because her training data didn't meet the requirements, Bao Zhuang left her alone and helped her with the training. After resuming the practice of serve receiving, Zhu Ting suddenly found her inspiration due to the muscle memory formed as the result of constant practice.

"Great job, Da Ting (nickname of Zhu Ting). The training of today can end in advance!" Bao Zhuang signalled to Zhu that she could rest.

"Coach Bao, could we practice a few more rounds?" Zhu Ting asked.

Seeing the coach confused, Zhu Ting explained, "I have practiced for so many days, but I didn't make progress until today, so I want to practice more to review the feeling. I am afraid of forgetting such feeling after having dinner and sleep."

In the meantime, Lang Ping was guiding the setters in the middle of the court. Hearing Zhu Ting's words, she couldn't help laughing in her heart, feeling that the unyielding spirit of Zhu Ting resembled that of her at young age.

Many similarities could be found between Zhu Ting and Lang Ping. They both practiced volleyball for five years before being selected to the national team at the age of 18. During her early days after joining the national team, Lang Ping also found her height somewhat undermining her ability of handling balls coming from relatively lower height. Yuan Weimin, her coach, made significant efforts to improve her all-round technical expertise and finally developed her into one of the "Best Outside Spikers." Thirty-five years later, it was the time for Lang Ping to help Zhu Ting.

5.

All thirteen members of the team for the Montreux Volley Masters were sitting in the rear part of the bus. While counting heads in the bus a moment ago, Lai Yawen whispered, "The team members led by Lang Ping were too young. Except for Zeng Chunlei and Yang Junjing, other members were all born in the 1990s."

Lang Ping waddled off the bus. Given the injuries from her athlete career, a long flight was always sheer torture for her waist, hips and legs. To minimize the effects of jet lag, she didn't sleep at all throughout the 11-hour flight. As a result, she felt quite sleepy when sitting in the dining room after hotel check-in.

"Yawen, please keep a close eye on them until they all have eaten their steaks as required." After hurrying up with her meal, Lang Ping whispered to Lai Yawen.

However, hardly had she gone out the dining room when the players began pleading with Coach Lai to be allowed to eat just half of their steaks. Given the fact that the players were very tired after the long journey, Lai Yawen relented and agreed with them. However, Lang Ping returned unexpectedly after finding that she had forgotten her room card when going upstairs. When seeing half steak was left in each player's plate, she became energetic again and watched them eat up the leftover steaks.

"You have all learned in the nutrition class that the fat content of steak is only 7%. It is really good for your health. You must eat it up. If I don't force you to eat them up, you will eat snacks in the room upstairs. As you know, snacks

During the Montreux Volley Masters, Lang Ping showed her childlike innocence by the Lake Geneva, Montreux. (Photo by Ma Yin)

can't offer you enough nutrition as needed."

The Chinese team, consisting of inexperienced players and a new coach, would attend the Montreux Volley Masters, the first competition for the Chinese team in 2014.

When adapting to the playing court the day before the match, Lang Ping called together her assistant coaches, An Jiajie and Wu Xiaolei, as well as the two medical doctors. Lang Ping assigned specific tasks to each of them. She also took this opportunity to have a rehearsal with them.

After deciding the jersey color of the Chinese team for their first match against Russia, Lang Ping immediately called An Jiajie and Wu Xiaolei with the phone in her room. "As they will wear white jerseys, let's wear red ones! Take your jerseys to my room and I will iron them for you. I don't hope we Chinese coaches stand there in clothes with wrinkles."

Lang Ping always had endless work to do. She never ignored any detail on and off the court.

6.

The day before the match, Lang Ping asked Ding Xia to go for a walk by the lake before dinner.

Ding Xia, who would represent the Chinese team for the first time, was really worried about not playing well the next day.

"Don't worry about that. I am sure you won't play well." To Ding Xia's surprise, Lang Ping added, "I know best your real competence. I just want you to widen your horizon by accumulating competition experience!"

At the night before the match, Lang Ping, Lai Yawen and An Jiajie respectively talked with the players under their charge. They focused on helping alleviate the pressure on these new players who would play for the national team for the first time. They understood that these players might be so eager to prove their capability through this competition that their performance might be hampered by distraction.

"We must help relieve their stress. They will certainly value the opportunity. However, they need our help and support."

Though it was just an ordinary invitational tournament, because Lang Ping determined to offer opportunities for new players to play on the court while seeking for better results, she needed to make more efforts together with other coaches to prepare for it.

Returning to the place where she rose to fame, Zhu Ting seemed worried about something. Originally a girl of few words, she became even more reticent. Lang Ping had been communicating with her before departure from China. Knowing that she didn't need to talk too much with this girl, Lang only asked Zhu the following questions and encouraged her to find the answers by herself: What's your goal for the tournament of this year since it's your second time to attend the event? What do you want to test, discover and improve through the competition?

Before the start of the match, Lang just emphasized that instead of caring too much about what others thought, Zhu should focus on pursuing what she desired.

As soon as Zhu Ting appeared on the playing court in the first round, coaches of other teams noticed that this young player began receiving serve. For any outside hitter in the world's volleyball circle, no matter how powerful her spike is, her attacking capability will be inevitably crippled as long as she is shouldered with the task of receiving serve. Seeing Zhu Ting had to take care of serve receiving, all opponents were extremely excited. They ultimately found a way to suppress and even restrict the strength of her.

From the first set, almost all the serves by the opponents were targeted at Zhu Ting. As the faults, deficient performance with receiving serve consumed too much of Zhu Ting's physical strength, and her attacking ability was also greatly undermined. Zhu Ting felt very depressed during these matches. However, due to the good preparation before the competition, the Chinese players kept calm despite fluctuation in performance.

Continuously being targeted by the opponents' serves, Zhu Ting tried to gradually adjust her mood. She realized that she needed to be patient enough if she really wanted to perform well in receiving serve. Under such unfavorable circumstances, she had no other choice but to try to receive every serve with all her efforts.

The Chinese team finished fourth with two wins and three losses. At the award ceremony, the top three teams were awarded trophies and medals, while the prize for the Chinese team was just a bottle of champagne.

The German women's volleyball team, the unexpected winner, rushed joyfully outside the stadium and frantically jumped into Lake Geneva for celebration. Seeing such scene, the Chinese players felt really depressed. At this moment, Lang Ping reminded them, "They have laid a solid foundation, but we don't. We have no other choice but to rely on ourselves and make more efforts to improve our skills."

7.

With the cooperation of veterans and inexperienced players, the Chinese team won a few matches that really helped boost morale, but also lost a few matches unexpectedly. Why couldn't the Chinese players give full play to their potential as they did in their daily routine training? Why did their performance fluctuate so dramatically?

The Chinese team lost to the Italian team in the match at Sassari. As the most powerful attacker of the Chinese team, Zhu Ting, under the defence by the opponents, only achieved a success rate of over 20 percent in this match. This was her lowest success rate since she represented the Chinese team to compete in international matches in 2013.

Because she failed to give full play to her attacking power, her confidence was undermined. Also, she only succeeded in rather limited number of blocking. Such poor performance frustrated her. After the match, Zhu Ting concluded that she didn't do herself justice in the match because she failed to fully control herself.

As the younger Chinese players were quite inexperienced, it was the time for the veteran ones to play their parts. Once at the team meeting, Xu Yunli, the most senior player of the team, helped her teammates better understand the relationship between 7 x 1 and 7:

"7 x 1 refers to the seven players of the starting lineup. After the training camp at Zhangzhou, each one of us has made progress. What's more, we have practiced various kinds of cooperation at Beilun training camp, which has really helped improve our competence. However, we fail to demonstrate obvious progress in teamwork during the competitions. Why? We haven't established real coordination and cooperation across the team, which needs our continuous practice and long-term accumulation."

During the tour matches of the Grand Prix, the Chinese team, with five wins and four losses, finished second and made it to the finals in Tokyo.

After learning that her team had secured a place in the finals, Coach Lang began to think about the lineup arrangement: Who needs a good rest first to alleviate exhaustion after previous competitions? Who has been plagued by injuries and illness and needs rehabilitation? Who is relatively less competent? Which new player is capable enough to compete on the court?

After deliberation, she made a surprising decision—Lai Yawen will take Zhu Ting, Hui Ruoqi and some other key players back to Beijing for adjustment and to prepare for the FIVB Volleyball Women's World Championship. In the meantime, she will lead the team mainly of substitute lineup to compete in Tokyo.

A year ago, Lang Ping didn't send the starting lineup to compete for the last match of the finals. This time she even planned to send the substitute lineup to the finals. People wondered why Lang Ping made such a decision. Striving for a good result would help the team boost their confidence, right?

Lang Ping didn't respond. She had her own plan.

She revealed her real intention to the players during their first meeting after their arrival in Tokyo. "We won't muddle along without clear target in the finals."

Lang Ping analyzed the opponents and prepared for the

matches in strict accordance with the same procedures and specifications as that for the starting lineup of key players. This made the substitute players really feel the pressure.

In the first match against Belgium, an emerging European team with strong attacking power, Lang Ping demanded that players on the court should be accountable and yell out to release pressure. However, during the match, no Chinese player could yell out.

The opponent of the second match was Brazil, which had won all the previous matches in the tour matches. When her attack was blocked by the opponents, the outside hitter Liu Xiaotong looked at Lang Ping helplessly. Lang Ping said, "Don't look at me. Zhu Ting is in Beijing. I have no substitute for you."

In the third set, Lang Ping lost her temper after the Chinese team lost to Japan 0-3, the host country team.

On the way from the stadium to the hotel, they all remained silent.

At the meeting after arriving at the hotel, Lang Ping asked the team members, "Do you know what the fighting spirit is?"

"Liu Xiaotong, don't always think you are still young. You are already 24 years old. I had already won three world championships when I was at your age! Are you still trying to find an alternative now? Of course, your ability really matters in your performance on the playing court. However, most importantly, you must be ready to forge ahead regardless of any challenge first. That is the so-called sense of mission."

Lang Ping's statement boosted the morale of all the team members including Liu Xiaotong.

When falling behind Turkey with 1-2 in their fourth set, the Chinese team turned the table by playing to their enormous potential.

Zeng Chunlei, with a determined look on her face, fulfilled her duty as the captain. Every time there came a ball difficult to handle, Liu Xiaotong always shouted to her teammates, "Pass it to me!" Yuan Xinyue, though a young player, helped the Chinese team reverse the situation by delivering good serves one after another.

The score was tied at 19-19 in the deciding set, and finally the Chinese team broke the stalemate to win this set with 21-19.

In response to the victory, Lang Ping shook her fist vigorously. Instead of the so-called achievement, what she really wanted was such a victory of real worth.

In 2014, it was the resilience shown by this lineup, half of which were substitutes that regained the confidence of their fans.

8.

After four weeks of fierce competitions at the Grand Prix, Lang Ping and her team returned to Beijing on August 25. She gave them two days off. The next day, instead of having a rest, she went to the training hall to instruct those key players who remained in Beijing and didn't attend the Grand Prix. On August 31, the whole team went to Beilun for the training camp before the FIVB Volleyball Women's World Championship. On September 4, she went alone from Beilun to Shenzhen to direct the competition of National B Team in the Asian Cup. On September 9, she returned to Beilun.

On September 10, while thinking about how to make better preparation for the FIVB Volleyball Women's World Championship, at the end of the morning training Lang Ping found in her mobile phone several missed calls from her elder sister.

"Unless something urgent, my sister usually doesn't call me when I'm working." Lang Ping felt something was wrong. Over the previous more than half a year, she was concerned about her father who had been in the hospital for seven months due to a sudden outbreak of cerebral infarction after China's Spring Festival. She remembered that her elder sister Lang Hong seemed quite busy when they talked over the phone two days ago. At that time, she worried about if her father was in a critical condition.

After she hurriedly called back, there came her sister's reply in a faint voice, "Xiaoping (Nickname of Lang Ping), dad passed away this morning."

Though psychologically prepared in advance, Lang Ping was immediately stunned by the sad news.

Lai Yawen and An Jiajie tried to comfort Lang Ping and persuade her to go home.

"My elder sister can take care of the family. I will go home in a few days!" Lang Ping made up her mind.

Every player of the team was trying to console their beloved coach. As words were more suitable at this moment, the team members sent Lang Ping what they wanted to say via WeChat respectively.

"Coach Lang, don't be too sad. We will go through all the difficulties together with you. I believe that your father hoped you will be happy and healthy. Please take care of yourself."

"Coach Lang, I just learned that your father passed away in the morning. For the sake of the honor and dignity of our national team, you are still keeping working as usual. Thank you for your devotion. I believe that your patient coaching will ultimately lead to our breakthrough! Coach Lang, hope you can restrain your grief and take care of yourself!"

Meanwhile, in the players' own WeChat group, the team captain Hui Ruoqi was the first to send message. "Fellows, what we can do now is to focus on training. Only by doing so can we alleviate Coach Lang's concerns over us. The FIVB Volleyball Women's World Championship will begin in over a week. We must overcome all the difficulties to fine-tune our skills and hold on straight to the end!"

The girls clenched their fists in agreement.

To adapt themselves to the schedule of the FIVB Volleyball Women's World Championship, the team changed their training sessions from the afternoon to the evening. To everyone's surprise, Lang Ping walked into the training hall on time as usual.

When the players were lined up, everyone kept their heads down, trying to avoid eye contact with Land Ping. However, they could hardly hold back their tears when Coach Lang calmly gave them instructions. As usual, after assigning the training plans to the players, Coach Lang warmed up with them together. During the training, she kept encouraging them and called a halt and made explanation when necessary as usual.

During the intervals between sets, she pushed the ball cart to another court. This time the players felt incredibly sad when looking at her from behind.

In the evening, Lang paid tribute to her father by sending a post on her Weibo.

"My father passed away this morning. He has always been proud of me, but I can do nothing but wish him peace in heaven." When writing down these words, Lang Ping could not stop crying.

After reading the post, Wei Qiuyue forwarded it with tears in her eyes. She expressed in the forwarded message the biggest wish of the national team at the moment. "We will do our best to work together in the upcoming FIVB Volleyball Women's World Championship!"

9.

The quadrennial FIVB Volleyball Women's World Championship was coming.

Lang Ping is Lai Yawen's mentor, teammate, partner and even close friend. They have witnessed the ups and downs of the Chinese women's volleyball team in the past 30 years. (Photo by Ma Yin)

This would be the sixth time for Lang Ping to attend the Championship in the past 32 years, and it was also the sixth time for Lai Yawen in the past 24 years. It would also be their third collaboration for this major event.

Lang Ping won many titles of world champions when she was an athlete. However, as one of the world's leading coaches, she hadn't led her team to win gold medal of any of the world's three major tournaments.

This time they would work together again. Would they make a breakthrough?

After the Chinese team's arrival in Bari, Italy, Wei Qiuyue delivered the last speech at the theory-discussing meeting before the competition and expressed the ambition to compete for a position on the podium.

"I think our team are promising. This allows me to look forward to a good result. So I take this chance to say what I think. Let's work together to achieve it!"

Though all the team members were aware of the tough challenges ahead for them, they applauded in response to this speech.

On the first match day, the Japanese women's volleyball team unexpectedly lost to Azerbaijan, a team with high stature in average. But Kimura Saori, the captain of the Japanese team, told Japanese reporters that the Japanese team would finish top of their group if they could upset China.

The fifth match day saw head-to-head competition between China and Japan. It was the first time the two teams met on such major event after the Chinese team lost to their Japanese counterpart at the 2012 London Olympic Games. Lang Ping was most concerned about the mentality of her players.

In the starting lineup of the Chinese team, five players experienced the Chinese team's failure at the 2012 London Olympic Games. They were Wei Qiuyue, Hui Ruoqi, Xu Yunli, Zeng Chunlei, and Yang Junjing. Zhu Ting and Chen Zhan, though newcomers, both had strong desire to defeat the Japanese team.

Lang Ping reminded them to treat the Japanese team just as an ordinary opponent, and only by doing so would the Chinese team perform well and lead to a good result.

The competition turned out to be quite fierce. The Chinese team got off to a good start by winning the first set. The Japanese team struggled to pull one set back. The Chinese team led all the way in the third set until 23-19 before an abrupt turn for the worse.

The Japanese team won the right to serve by gaining a point with a first-round attack, which was followed by two consecutive serves by Ishii Yuki, an up-and-coming young player of Japan, resulting in the Chinese team's fault of serve receiving. Wang Huimin was sent onto receiving serve. She managed to dig the ball up. However, the Chinese team's free ball was killed by the opponent.

After scoring five points in a row, the Japanese team instantly surpassed their Chinese counterpart and maintained such good momentum until they won the set point. The loss of two consecutive sets pushed the Chinese team on the verge of failure.

Early in the crucial fourth set, Xu Yunli was hit in the face by a hard spike from Ishii Yuki. The medical doctor rushed into the field with an ice bag. When Lang Ping was considering substitution, Xu Yunli was seen trying to stand up and showing that she could hold on. She wiped away tears and continued the match despite her red and swollen eyes.

Inspired by Xu Yunli's spirit of perseverance, the Chinese team, amid the warm applause of the spectators, finally kept the competition under their control. With the deciding set ended at 15-11, the Chinese team outplayed their Japanese counterpart 3-2, finishing first in the group. The players hugged each other in celebration of the victory. For the Chinese team that were preparing for the 2016 Rio Olympic Games, the significance of this hard-won victory was beyond the victory itself.

10.

On the final day of the tournament in Bari, the Chinese team competed with the host country team for the first place in the big group.

Before this match, the Chinese team had been exhausted both physically and mentally after fierce competition and long journeys across different venues. It was already midnight after the Chinese team finished the match and got everything ready. The whole team got up early in the next morning and set off. They spent most of the daytime on the road before they finally arrived late in the afternoon. They couldn't have a rest as they got on the bus not long after they got off the plane, having stayed in the tight space for long hours.

This would be the third-time encounter between China and Italy in 2014. As the host, the Italian team fully showed their determination to win this match.

In Bari's competition venue, which was not a large one, all seats were occupied for the first time since the start of the tournament. The overwhelming waves of sound could be felt as soon as one entered the venue. Cheerleaders were cheering in unison and all spectators were singing and dancing to the tune.

The well-prepared Chinese team got into the state quickly and won the first set before the local spectators' passion were motivated and the opponent woke up to reality. However, a detail during the match highlighted the host's determination to win the first place of the group. As the official review result approved the success of the challenge by the Chinese team, the referee amended the judgment by declaring that the Chinese team scored a point. However, under the pressure by the defiant Italian head coach Marco Bonita, the referee changed his mind and showed a yellow card to Lang Ping when she argued for reasonable explanation. Lang Ping, who was praised for the accurate judgment, was so angry about the referee's decision that she couldn't help laughing.

From the second half of the second set, factors both on and off the court came into play. As a result, the Chinese team narrowly lost to the host country team, with their eight consecutive wins ending at 1-3. The Italian team grabbed the first place of the group as they hoped.

Since Lang Ping had gone through so many challenges, she wasn't supposed to be greatly affected by this failure. Unexpectedly, she couldn't go on with the conversation during the media interview after the match. Covering her face with her hands, she walked quickly to the bathroom. Several female reporters followed her. In front of the bathroom mirror, Lang Ping was wiping her tears with a tissue.

When walking out of the bathroom, Lang Ping explained to these reporters, "I feel sad mainly because I am worried that this failure will frustrate our hardworking players."

11.

The goal of the Chinese team before the FIVB Volleyball Women's World Championship was to gain their access by ranking among the top six.

Brazil, Dominica, Italy, Russia and the United States would be the formidable opponents ahead. How far could the Chinese team go?

The Chinese team were completely outgunned 0-3 in the competition against Brazil that ranked the first place in the global ranking. The Chinese team had to be eliminated from the tournament if they couldn't upset their next opponent, Dominica.

On the night of October 9, 2014, the Chinese team faced their toughest challenges at this event.

Dominica, by leveraging their strength in hard spike, won the first and second sets consecutively. This almost extinguished the hope of the Chinese team to win this match.

In the third set, Lang Ping was quite active in arranging substitutions and every player on the court was trying her best. Despite their efforts, the Chinese team still lagged behind. With 20-17, the Dominican team were likely to win the match soon.

At this critical moment, Hui Ruoqi managed to defend the hard spike by Bethania De La Cruz De Pena, one of the spikers of the opponent. Zeng Chunlei gained a point through counterattack, successfully curbing the opponent's momentum of continuously scoring points. The attack by Zeng Chunlei and Zhu Ting, combined with the blocking by

Yang Junjing, helped the Chinese team surpass the opponent by consecutively winning four points.

The competition was very fierce. With a successful attack by Zhu Ting, the Chinese team managed to obtain the set point with 24-23. At the critical moment, Xu Yunli and Hui Ruoqi formed a two-person block and blocked the power attack by Dominica's No. 17 Gina Altagracia Mambru Casilla from zone 2. As a result, the Chinese team won this set. Just as the Chinese members were excitedly celebrating the turnaround, Xu Yunli was found lying on the ground in agony, with one of her ankles severely sprained.

Upon the arrival of the ambulance, Xu Yunli was wheeled away on a stretcher.

With the match going on, the Chinese team were giving full play to their potential.

Already on the brink of failure, they found nothing could stand on their way! Every point they scored made them feel determined and more confident. The Dominican team that had come so close to a 3-0 victory, on the contrary, became somewhat hesitant for they had lost their best opportunity.

In the fourth set, the match was tied at 23-23. At this critical moment, Zeng Chunlei and Zhu Ting scored two points consecutively, respectively through first-round attack and counterattack from zone 2. This helped the Chinese team win this set.

The deciding set was still very fierce, with Dominica leading 11-10 before the score was tied at 12-12. Zeng Chunlei, through her serves, created two opportunities for direct spike, which were seized respectively by Yuan Xinyue and Wei Qiuyue.

The Chinese team ultimately got the match point!

Zeng Chunlei walked towards the service zone. With her back to the court, she tried to calm down. Then she turned around and kept her eyes on An Jiajie, who was sitting on the team bench, for instructions on the expected landing point to serve. The Chinese coach and the player would usually have such exchange before serving. Sometimes they shared the same opinion, while sometimes they held different ideas. However, this time the gesture shown by Coach An was exactly the same as what Zeng Chunlei planned!

Remembering the tips, Zeng bounced the ball to prepare, then she tossed the ball, jumped and hit the ball. She made a perfect serve! The ball flew over the net in a graceful arc and was grounded right between two Dominican players. The Chinese team scored the winning point.

As soon as the ball that secured the victory was grounded on the court, Lang Ping, Lai Yawen and An Jiajie hugged together and the girls couldn't hold back their tears anymore. Led by Yuan Xinyue, they laughed, shouted and cheered. Their loud cheers echoed through the night of Milan.

12.

Back to the hotel, Lang Ping saw several players sitting on the sofa on the first-floor lobby to wait for the upcoming match. Even though the team members were allowed to relax themselves, they had something on their minds. Of course, when it came to Italy, the girls surely wanted to do shopping and enjoy local foods. However, at this moment, their greatest wish was that Brazil would beat Dominica so that the Chinese team could rank among the final four.

With the Brazilian team being close to winning the

match, those Chinese girls stood up and hugged each other, saying "we are now the final four." Upstairs in the room, Lang Ping turned on her computer and began to prepare for the semi-final competition with Italy.

Xu Yunli, though injured, was assigned with the task to help Yuan Xinyue hone her skills. By watching videos together and explaining details of each movement, Xu instructed Yuan on how to judge the pass by the Italian setter and helped her analyze the skill differences between various attacks, telling her which spiker would be more trustworthy by the setter at critical moments involving key points.

Entrusted with this great mission all of a sudden, Yuan Xinyue had to master all these key tips within 24 hours and put them into practices in the upcoming competition. Before going to bed, seeing Yuan lying in bed but still analyzing the skills on an iPad, Xu wished that she could pass on her strength to the hard-working girl.

The night before the semi-final, Yuan Xinyue, holding the iPad, had a dream about this crucial match. In her dream, the Chinese team performed exceptionally well. In her dream, she did a good job though it was her first time to be in the starting lineup for such an important match. The Chinese team won!

Before the match, Yuan Xinyue did not dare to tell anyone about the dream. She was afraid that the dream would lose its magic power once it was revealed in advance.

Brazil, who had won 11 matches consecutively, lost 0-3 to the United States before semi-final began. The elimination of Brazil, one of the favorites, was a surprise for both the Chinese and Italian teams that would soon vie for another place in the final that night. However, given their different positions, they felt excited for different reasons.

As the host, Italy looked forward to winning the championship again by taking their home turf advantage. In 2002, the Italian team led by Marco Bonita won their first world championship at the FIVB Volleyball Women's World Championship. Twelve years later, the event was held in Europe again. With extremely high morale, the Italian team were determined to win the championship again. Their most powerful rival was no doubt the Brazilian team who won Olympic Champion two times and enjoyed No. 1 world ranking.

Throughout the Championship, the host country team would prefer not to meet Brazil before entering the finals, and it would be ideal to compete against China at the semi-finals, as the Chinese team mainly consisted of young players.

Right before the semi-finals, news came that the Brazilian team had been eliminated from the event. What a heaven-sent chance for the Italian team to win the champion!

At the night of October 11 in 2014, the 12,000 seats of Milan stadium were all occupied. The whole stadium burst into waves of uproar and shouts, which quickened the heartbeats of everyone present. When the Italian national anthem was played before the match, the Italians, whether they were acquaintances or not, all held tight their compatriots of adjacent seats with arms, and sang the same song. At the end of the anthem, the Italians present all shouted "hey" loudly and together, impressing the world.

The gambling companies were overwhelmingly in favor of the Italian team before the match, predicting that Italy would win a complete victory of 3-0.

Compared with the ambitious host country team, the Chinese team, who had managed to make the final four, had no psychological burden before the final match. With the mentality of "one point earned, one step further", the Chinese team performed with ease from the very beginning. A positive mentality naturally gave a better play to the skills. Before the Italian team fully focused on the match, the well-prepared Chinese team had won the first two sets.

The Italian players, aware that the victory was slipping away, pulled themselves together to tap their enormous potential. With adjusted lineup, the Italian team won the third set by taking advantage of the Chinese team's minor faults.

The competition in the critical fourth set became white-hot, with scores seesawed all along. When this set saw the two teams tied at 23-23, the Chinese team had failed to turn match point into victory for three times due to the strong resistance of the Italian team.

The competition was so fierce that any minor mistake by any player might lead to failure. At such critical moment, all the players were forging ahead with care despite the difficulties!

28-28! Yuan Xinyue yelled as she scored a key point by successfully delivering a high quick spike. Then, Hui Ruoqi tried her best to score the match point by a hard spike!

30-28! China beat Italy 3-1 to reach the World Championship's final.

It was after 16 years that the Chinese team again reached the final of the World Championship. Last time, Lang Ping was also the head coach!

Despite her injury, Xu Yunli, walking on crutches, rushed onto the court to join the cheering team.

13.

With the coveted world championship within reach, Lang Ping encouraged her players to fight for championship by overcoming difficulties and never giving up.

Realizing that the final would begin a dozen of hours later, the players knew it was time to stay calm and concentrate on the upcoming competition. However, these Chinese girls who reached the pinnacle of their career for the first time, could hardly calm down soon. They had overcome too many difficulties for this day. In the initial phase, they won eight matches in a row, which earned them a place among the top six. Then they staged a comeback to become the final four. After that, they entered the final by outplaying Italy. While lying on the bed, the girls still couldn't help recalling the matches and celebrations...

It was destined to be a sleepless night.

To better prepare for the competition against the U.S. team, Lang Ping hardly slept a wink. The next morning, she showed the video to the team, and after lunch break, she held the preparation meeting. The last match day of the World Championship passed very quickly.

It was rather a pity that the Chinese players hadn't got fully prepared for the final of the Championship, and lost to the U.S. team.

For Zeng Chunlei, it was a great pity that the Chinese team lost in the final. She said: "After the semi-final, we were indulged in the joy brought by the victory. We couldn't calm ourselves down for the final. I believe this is why we lost to the U.S. team."

At the award ceremony, staring at the champion trophy awarded to the U.S. women's volleyball team, the Chinese girls deeply regretted the loss of the expected championship.

CHAPTER THREE

2015

The strong one is born out of challenges

It was from the night when the Chinese team won the silver medal that Lang Ping began to reflect on the team's performance during the 2014 FIVB Volleyball Women's World Championship.

Was it a pity that the Chinese team let the championship slip away?

Could they win the championship if given another chance?

Or was it a big surprise that the Chinese team went all the way from the sixth place to the final?

The girls not only won the matches that they should win, but also won the matches that they are not sure if they could win. However, could they still win all these matches if they fight the same opponents again? Lang Ping kept asking herself these questions.

Finishing runner-up didn't mean that China was a world-class team. It only showed that the Chinese team were heading in the right direction and could keep going. However, the Chinese team would be very likely to fall behind if they failed to solve those problems found in training and in the competitions.

Back in Beijing, Lang Ping was still racking her brains. She kept asking herself: how can I find a way to keep Zhu Ting in a better shape? How can we find and train new liberos for our team? Could Zhang Changning, Ding Xia and other young players make progress as expected after this year's training?

On December 9, 2014, the wind was howling in Beijing. On this day, Wei Qiuyue and her mother, all in down coats, departed from Beijing Capital International Airport for Chicago, where Wei would receive a debridement operation on her knees. This meant that they would have to spend this winter in snowy Chicago.

One day later is Lang Ping's 54th birthday. On her birthday, Lang Ping received a diary with gold cover.

Bidding Farewell to 2014, a year full of challenges and surprises, Lang Ping wrote down on the title page the following words: 2015, try my best!

1.

On January 28, 2015, the Chinese team led by Lang Ping began the third year of their preparation for the 2016 Rio Olympic Games.

Sometimes, it felt like that time flew and that one could hardly find time for a rest, let alone taste the sweetness of achievement. But sometimes, it seemed that time went very slowly, and these days and weeks witnessed the arduous journey of this team. They had come a long way before realizing it.

Due to the two-year efforts, the Chinese team now regained their vitality and developed themselves into an extremely competitive team capable of addressing various challenges. Thanks to Lang Ping's strategy of building "a strong national team," the team had taken their preliminary shape. A group of enterprising young coaches and promising young players had been identified, selected and well trained. After taking part in the world-class matches in 2014, the team members had gradually adapted themselves to their respective roles. During the process of catching up with their leading counterparts, the team members had developed good habits of continuously learning from the best.

On the first day at the training hall, Lang Ping looked all around the "battlefield" as usual and then winked at Lai, saying, "Don't forget to add seats."

Lai Yawen got her message at once.

In the list of the national team's training camp in 2015, "the Old Pal" (Lai Yawen usually called Lang Ping in this way) selected a total of 26 players. In the first-phase training camp in Beijing, Lang Ping planned to gather 22 players, including 5 libero candidates, which was very rare in the history of the training camp for the national team. As a really considerate coach, Lai Yawen had already added seats to the training venue.

On the first day of the training camp for the 22 players, the spacious volleyball hall was a bit crowded. At Lai Yawen's request, two more benches were placed along the wall.

It might be the first time in the history of the Chinese team that a total of 22 players participated in the training, which was divided into two rows. With so many new members, the players had to line up according to their heights.

"You are the most promising athletes with the greatest potential across China. For the first-phase training camp, we hope to find players who are capable enough to join the national team for the 2016 Rio Olympic Games. In this process, everyone had the chance to show her ability. This period won't last too long, because there are too many participants here and it was hard to pay enough attention to everyone. We will ultimately select sixteen or seventeen players for our two major tasks this year, the Asian Women's Volleyball Championship and the FIVB Volleyball Women's World Cup."

Taking Yuan Xinyue as an example again, Lang Ping encouraged the new players and said, "Everything is possible."

2.

Lang Ping and Chen Zhonghe met again in Zhangzhou in March 2015.

Whenever they met, Lang Ping would play jokes on Chen Zhonghe, and Chen would always respond with a big grin.

In 1979, Chen Zhonghe, 22 years old, went to report to the Chinese team by train, and for the first time met Lang Ping who was only 19. On Chen's first day of training, Yuan Weimin arranged this skillful young man to practice knocking with Lang Ping, one of Yuan's most favorite athletes. In those years, Lang Ping, a cheerful Beijing girl, often teased Chen, the shy lad from Southern Fujian. However, compared with the senior players, Lang Ping didn't carry her joke too far with her young coach. After all, she was three years younger than Chen Zhonghe.

Right now, Lang Ping and Chen Zhonghe were warmly exchanging their recent situation, and the players started to take a break. Coming from the other side of the court, Zhu Ting and Li Tong were talking very excitedly. Before taking their seats, it seemed that Li Tong said something, which made Zhu Ting play a dramatic trick on him. She put her arms around his neck as if she wanted to lock his throat. Li Tong then cooperated with her trick, pretending to be frightened and begged for mercy. With a self-satisfied smirk on her face, Zhu Ting said, "Call me Big Sister and I'll let you go."

Lang Ping and Chen Zhonghe laughed at this scene, which made them recall the past. They together experienced the ups and downs of the elder generation of the Chinese team and enjoyed the joy of success together. Now, over 30 years later, they saw from these young players their good old days.

They devoted the best period of their youth to the target of "claiming five successive world championships." As soon as the target was fulfilled, in 1986 Lang Ping retired as an

Lang Ping and Chen Zhonghe have known each other for 40 years. They worked together for the Chinese women's volleyball team, which laid a solid foundation for their 40-year friendship. (Photo by Ma Yin)

athlete and chose to study abroad, while Chen Zhonghe returned to work as a coach at Fujian Provincial team.

In 1995 when Lang Ping returned to China to set up a team of coaches for the Chinese team, the first candidate that came to her mind was Chen Zhonghe, a dedicated veteran who knew the Chinese team very well. As soon as she arrived in Beijing, Lang Ping called Chen Zhonghe and said, "Zhonghe, your child is still young, and I can fully understand if you don't want to leave your family behind. After all, this job will last at least two years." Chen Zhonghe answered without hesitation, "I'm in. You have come all this way back, so don't worry about me! As long as you need my support, I shall be glad to cooperate with you."

As Lang Ping's chief assistant coach, Chen worked with Lang Ping for four years.

In 2001, when the new Chinese team were about to be formed, Lang Ping recommended Chen Zhonghe to be the head coach because he knew the team better than anybody else.

Time was the best witness to their friendship. The story of their friendship had also become one of the popular anecdotes throughout the 40-year history of the Chinese team.

"Zhu Ting is really like what you were at your youthful age!" Chen Zhonghe, who cherished talent, fixed his eyes on Zhu Ting. "Coach Lang, if you train her well, the Chinese team are more likely to rise again!"

Since Lang Ping retired in 1986, the Chinese team had been looking for a new leader or a successor of the title of the "Iron Hammer" in the next generation. After 30 years, the successor finally appeared.

After serving as the head coach of the Chinese team, Lang Ping focused on training Zhu Ting and Yuan Xinyue in 2013 and 2014 respectively. In the third year of preparation for the 2016 Rio Olympic Games, the 20-year-old Zhang Changning was expected to become one of the new leading players. Therefore, in 2015, Lang and her coaching staff decided to focus on training Zhang Changning. Lang Ping had very high expectation on them. However, at this moment, the even higher priority was given to honing the skills of the substitutes while basically determining the starting lineup. Lang aimed to bridge the skill gap between the substitutes and the starting lineup, so that anyone of them could take responsibility when needed.

Under the guidance of Lang Ping, Zhu Ting, Yuan Xinyue and Zhang Changning made rather rapid progress and became the core members of the Chinese team. In 2015, they collaborated with each other for the first time in the FIVB Volleyball Women's World Cup, helping the Chinese team win the championship. (Photo by Li Zhiyan)

3.

In 2015, the Chinese women's volleyball team embarked on a new journey starting from the Asian Women's Volleyball Championship.

Lang Ping still remembered their experience at the Asian Women's Volleyball Championship held on September two years ago, where the Chinese team were thwarted at the very beginning.

In the past 20 months, no one had ever asked her if the Chinese team's finishing fourth at the Asian Women's Volleyball Championship was out of her expectation. She was also never puzzled by this failure. She believed that the only thing she should do was to face the failure, analyze the weaknesses and try to improve.

This failure must have taught the Chinese team a lesson. From then on, the Chinese team could always win their competitions whether it was against Thailand or South Korea. What's more, this new team had then won the silver medal at the 2014 FIVB Volleyball Women's World Championship. However, as the old saying goes, "one must stand up from where he once fell." This time, the Asian Women's Volleyball Championship was the same case for Lang Ping and the Chinese players.

This time, the event went on as it did 20 months ago. The Chinese team did not meet any strong rival from the group stage to the semi-final stage. At the semi-final, the Chinese team would compete against the Thailand team, who were the host country team last time and the defending champion this time.

The day before the semi-finals, the atmosphere of the Chinese team was somewhat serious.

The Chinese team had made a lot of preparations for this match, both technically and mentally. As the match was not far off, certainly everyone was eager to win but was not quite sure about it. After all, this was a one-off match. Given the opponent's unique skills and the excellent performance since the beginning of the match, what if the Chinese team failed to perform as well as expected?

Lang Ping did not say much when she gathered the team before the training, but asked everyone to brace up and make good use of the one-hour training at the competition venue by repeating the drills according to the technical characteristics shown by the Thailand team in their previous six rounds of matches. She asked the team members to be highly focused and just run forward instead of looking around when the practice item was alternated.

What were the players of the Chinese team worried about when they would meet the Thailand team again in the semi-finals of the Asian Women's Volleyball Championship?

The Thailand team always played at a fast pace that the Chinese team found it difficult to deal with. What if the Chinese players still failed to catch up with the speed of their counterparts even after so many efforts had been made in practices? What should the Chinese players do if they fell behind? What to do next if the Chinese team failed in the first set? What if the Chinese team lost two sets in a row? These were their worries.

Lang Ping thoroughly analyzed these problems one after another and instructed the players on how to adjust their mentality if such a situation really happened.

Lang Ping also encouraged the players, telling them that

there would be other possibilities during the match. For example, how should they go on after winning two sets in a row? Or if they were at the deciding 5th set, how should they play?

With all the plans in place, the Chinese girls finally became relieved.

They realized they must try to focus on winning every point because no matter how eagerly they wanted to win the match, they had to score points, one by one.

After the first set of the semi-final between China and Thailand was tied at 22, the Chinese team lost three points in a row. As for the last two points, Zhang Changning, a young player who substituted Hui Ruoqi, tried to attack but got blocked, and then she tried to spike but failed. The players of the Thailand team excitedly hugged together to celebrate. The originally passionate atmosphere at the Tianjin host venue suddenly became solemn.

In the second set, facing their Thailand counterparts that had completely relaxed themselves, the Chinese players became so nervous that they lost three points in a row right at the beginning of this set.

The Chinese team managed to save the fourth serve by the opponent and Zhu Ting scored a point by a powerful attack. It was the turn of Yang Junjing to serve. She encouraged herself as she walked towards the service zone, hoping that she could make her contributions when the team were under such unfavorable condition.

It was time for every Chinese player to try their best.

At the second technical timeout, the Chinese team pulled ahead 16-15. It took a set and a half for the Chinese players to gradually relax themselves and find their rhythm.

The competition continued, although the scores were rather close, the Chinese players performed much better than the previous set.

The Chinese team won the second set 25-22 by consecutively scoring several key points.

The third set was firstly tied at 7-7, but later the Chinese team got the upper hand and won this set 25-10.

In the fourth set, the Thailand team staged a comeback. At the beginning of this set, they lagged behind, but they then gave a full play to their unique skills. Unexpectedly, the Thailand team surpassed the Chinese team by scoring 6 points in a row. At the critical moments, what really mattered was players' willpower.

The Chinese fans became nervous again. When the Chinese team requested timeout this time, the hands of the Chinese girls were tightly clasped.

It was the high spike by Zhu Ting that suppressed the opponent's momentum of scoring points consecutively. She roared and shook her fist as the ball was grounded on the playing court. In this set, the Chinese team got equalized, led, got equalized again and then was surpassed by the opponent. It was again the hard spike by Zhu Ting that helped the Chinese team win this set 25-23. As a result, the Chinese team won the match 3-1!

At the moment of victory, all the Chinese players sitting on the bench rushed into the court. The 12 players hugged each other tightly. Although more than half of the team members didn't experience the failure 20 months ago, they could feel the significance and value of this victory by going over how the Chinese team endured hardships and forged ahead despite adversity.

Through excellent teamwork, China overcame a series of great challenges at the Asian Women's Volleyball Championship, and finally regained the long-awaited Asian championship after upsetting South Korea led by Kim Yeon-koung with 3-1 in the final.

4.

One day in June, after a day of training in Beijing, assistant coach Wu Xiaolei suddenly said to Li Tong, "Have you noticed that it's a bit tough to outplay these girls in the drill competition?"

The third year after Lang Ping served again as the head coach of the Chinese women's volleyball team, these girls had made so rapid progress that even the male coaches would be exhausted after a day of intensive training with them.

Talking about the FIVB Volleyball Women's World Cup to be held two months later, both Wu Xiaolei and Li Tong believed that the Chinese team would be capable of performing well at the event. Such upward momentum of the Chinese team was later fully embodied in the FIVB World Grand Prix. As the Brazilian team, the host country team of the Rio Olympic Games, wouldn't participate in the FIVB Volleyball Women's World Cup, the international volleyball community had higher expectation for the Chinese team who were the runner-up of the FIVB Volleyball Women's World Championship, predicting that they would make a difference at the Women's World Cup.

The FIVB Volleyball Women's World Cup would be the most critical event for the Chinese team in 2015.

As required by the FIVB Volleyball Women's World Cup, the total number of registered players for each team was 14. Therefore, 14 out of the 16 players training in Beilun would appear on the final list. The final decision wasn't unveiled until August 17, the day before the Chinese team departed for the FIVB Volleyball Women's World Cup.

Unexpectedly, the second one rejected turned out to be Hui Ruoqi, the captain of the team, which sounded like an April Fool's joke to everyone. After all, Hui Ruoqi was widely considered as a model of the Chinese team, enjoying full attendance in the previous few years. After experiencing sudden cardiac discomfort during the training camp in Beilun, Hui Ruoqi went to the hospital, where she was diagnosed as having serious arrhythmia. Group consultation by medical experts from Beijing was arranged as soon as possible, but the results turned out to be not optimistic. For the sake of her health, the Volleyball Sports Management Center under the General Administration of Sport of China finally decided not to include her in the Chinese team for the FIVB Volleyball Women's World Cup.

During the training session before departure, Lang Ping asked the team members to face up to the difficulties bravely and believe in the power of teamwork. However, the girls, depressed under so huge psychological pressure, could hardly feel refreshed.

At the end of the training, Lang Ping called everyone together as usual. It was her last "review" of the team before the Herculean task. Over the past three years, Lang Ping had been accustomed to seeing Hui Ruoqi standing in a prominent position of the first row. This time, when Lang Ping looked in that direction without seeing the captain, the sense of grief struck her, but she insisted on briefing the players on her expectations. Back to her seat to pack for the trip, all of a sudden, she paused for a moment, then put down her backpack, and hurried to the cloak room.

The assistant coaches thought she went to fetch something and were going to help her, but the tears in her eyes silenced them.

Fortunately, she regained her control soon. She quickly adjusted her mood and go on making preparations.

5.

China met Serbia in the opening match of the FIVB

Due to Hui Ruoqi's temporary absence, Zhang Changning (left) had to serve as one of the key players of the Chinese team for the FIVB Volleyball Women's World Cup. Less than 20 years old then, she didn't have enough confidence in herself. Yang Junjing (right) and other senior players tried to help her alleviate pressure on and off the court. (Photo by Li Zhiyan)

Volleyball Women's World Cup.

The Serbian women's volleyball team, dubbed the "New Army of Europe" in the previous decade, became unrivaled with the rise of "genius girl" Tijana Boskovic who was born in 1997.

Under the pressure of the opponent's powerful attack, the Chinese team lost the first set 19-25, and fell behind again 10-15 in the second set.

When her team lagged behind by a large margin in the second set, Lang Ping requested substitutions. Seeing Ding Xia and Liu Yanhan, two unknown young players, the opponent thought the Chinese team were giving up.

While rushing to the courtside with the number plate for substitution card in her hands, Ding Xia had only one idea in mind. She had to throw caution to the wind!

The two substitutes inspired the whole team with their passion.

Every time the team gained a crucial point, Ding Xia would rush around half part of the court to celebrate. Liu Yanhan raised her hands and shouted with excitement as her power attack pierced through the solid defence of the Serbian team. The high-decibel shouts of Yuan Xinyue echoed in the court again. Zhu Ting, the leading figure of the Chinese team, was well supported by her teammates.

The Serbian players seemed overwhelmed by the passion and courage of Chinese players. Due to a simple mistake by Boskovic in her attack, the Chinese team leveled the score and strode toward victory.

The final two points of the fourth set were scored by Zhu Ting. For this, the TV station also broadcasted a specially produced short video titled "How the 'Iron Hammer' Coaches Her Successors for Her Motherland".

Ultimately, the Chinese team struggled to overcome the Serbian team 3-1 at the opening match of the FIVB Volleyball Women's World Cup by turning the match around.

As the coaches shook hands on the center line, Zoran Terzic looked at Lang Ping perplexedly and muttered in English, "What is the tactics you use?"

Lang Ping shrugged. "Honestly, I don't know."

The next day, perhaps stimulated by losing a match even without knowing what was going on, Zoran Terzic led the Serbian team to a landslide victory over the hotly-tipped U.S. team.

Wasn't it a godsend for the other favorite team, the Chinese team?

However, to seize opportunity, people were apt to be too eager for success. In the third round of the event, China met the U.S.

At the pre-match preparation meeting, in addition to technical details, Lang Ping repeatedly reminded her players of adjusting their attitudes. "Treat it just like a normal match. Relax," she said.

"We all have to concentrate on the competition, or otherwise we will be distracted. I hope to win, but I'm also afraid of losing the match," said Yang Junjing, the middle-blocker who attended the FIVB Volleyball Women's World Cup for the second time, "This is especially the case when I fail to play as smoothly as expected, and I could not accept the fact that others might perform better than me."

In fact, the Americans could hardly calm down either. Shortly after the start of the match, the U.S. coach Karch Kiraly challenged the referee by continuously asking for official review for three times. Kiraly refused to give up even after his challenges failed. With strong desire to win, the U.S. team launched aggressive attack one round after another by virtue of hard power. Overwhelmed by the attack, all Chinese players were quite anxious.

Under the increasing pressure from the U.S. team, the Chinese team lost rallies at an astonishing speed. In the third set, when the U.S. team scored the winning point, the Chinese girls were frustrated and stunned. Why the match that they had prepared for so long a time ended so quickly? The girls were outplayed 0-3.

Yuan Xinyue cried. Zhang Changning kept her eyes straight on the court. Zhu Ting was expressionless. The captain Zeng Chunlei, a merry girl, looked quite upset... They all felt it was their faults that led to the failure.

Back at the hotel, seeing the team's low morale, Lang Ping reminded them that the FIVB Volleyball Women's World Cup had just started and there were still eight rounds of competition ahead. She said, "As we've made mistakes, the initiative isn't in our hands. Next, we have to wait for the other teams to make mistakes. However, we can't afford any mistake."

6.

In the fourth round of the FIVB Volleyball Women's World Cup, China led 2-1 into the fourth set with South Korea. Unfortunately, not long after the crucial fourth set began, China's key player Zhu Ting got injured after executing the blocking action because she stepped on the foot of South Korea's No. 8 player Kim Hee-Jin that stepped across the center line. Zhu Ting, with her right ankle injured, fell to the ground. At that moment, all the Chinese concerned were taken aback. Hui Ruoqi already missed the FIVB Volleyball Women's World Cup because of her illness. If the injury would prevent Zhu Ting from continuing the match, the strength of the Chinese team would be greatly weakened.

Lang Ping, with a calm expression, glanced at Zhu Ting who was sitting on the bench for emergency treatment by the medical doctor. She found Zhu, instead of removing all her protective gear, still trying to stretch her ankle and preparing to return to the court.

When Lang Ping was young at about the same age of Zhu, she also sprained her right ankle once. The injury happened when she took part in a match held in China on behalf of the Chinese team. During the warm-up before the match, she jumped up for spike but stepped on a mop that wasn't put in the right place. As the match was about to start, the medical doctor of the Chinese team rushed to deal with the sprain. But Lang Ping refused as she felt that she could bear it, and asked the doctor to tie her right ankle tightly to the extent that almost no pain could be felt. Nearly two decades later, during a business trip to Russia, her right ankle was injured again and she had it examined at a local hospital. With her X-ray film in hand, the Russian doctor asked her, "You once had a fracture here, right?"

Lang Ping had more than one bone fracture that hadn't been treated properly or were left to recover by themselves. Lang Ping never told her players how she had persisted in spite of injuries. Lang Ping hoped that better medical equipment and well-developed science and technology could improve players' quality of life, and maximize their athlete career. Therefore, she always emphasized that good health was of top priority. Any injury must be reported for early care and treatment in case the injury worsens.

But for this moment, should she let Zhu go back to the court with her ankle injured?

When South Korea rallied to overtake China with 14-13, Zhu Ting asked Lang Ping for substitution. To make breakthroughs in the FIVB Volleyball Women's World Cup, the Chinese team couldn't afford to lose even this one set, let alone a match.

Amid the applause of the spectators, Zhu Ting, holding high the number plate of substitution, walked to the side of the court. She limped into the court and stood on her familiar position. After she rejoined the team, the setter Shen Jingsi passed the ball to her. She jumped high again as usual, trying to ground the ball at the place that was the most difficult for the opponent players to defend. However, it was not the same case as before. Every time she fell on the ground, the injured ankle had to bear the huge impact. There was a flash of pain difficult to hide on her face at the moment, which made the Chinese coaches, players and volleyball fans nervous.

The South Korean team were still trying every means to compete against the Chinese team, keeping a four-point lead at 21-17. As for the remaining points of this set, it seemed that the determination of the Chinese team to win the first place had to be tested again. Though injured, Zhu Ting and her teammates passed the test.

Ultimately, the Chinese team won 25-23! Many Chinese players couldn't help crying when the victory came.

It was neither the fierce competition nor the powerful

opponent that moved them into tears. Instead, what really mattered were the difficulties that had to be addressed, the pain and bitterness that must be experienced and endured. Encouragingly, the Chinese team got through it.

7.

Then the Chinese women's volleyball team moved to Nagoya for the competition of the final stage of the FIVB Volleyball Women's World Cup.

Since Lang Ping came to Japan for the FIVB Volleyball Women's World Cup in 1981, she had attended the event five times in the past 34 years. According to the agreement signed by the FIVB and Japan in 1977, the following events would be held in Japan forever. This meant that during each event the Chinese team had to travel to three or four cities for competitions. Therefore, Lang Ping had been to the major cities of Japan more than two or three times. Of course, she was most familiar with the stadiums of those cities.

In Nagoya, the 2015 FIVB Volleyball Women's World Cup entered the most critical phase. Since losing their initiative due to their loss to the U.S. team in the third round, the Chinese team had changed their target to accomplish each and every task steadily and wait for opportunities.

Serbia upset Russia 3-2 in the seventh round, and Russia outplayed the United States 3-0 in the ninth round. If China could defeat the last two opponents, Russia and Japan, they would win the champion!

At 3 p.m. local time, September 5, 2015, the Chinese team met the Russian team, their 10th opponent at this FIVB Volleyball Women's World Cup. The winner of this match would be definitely closer to the championship, while the loser would be eliminated from the title race.

It was the first time that 28-year-old Yan Ni attended such a world-class match. The night before the match, after studying the match videos of the Russian team at the meeting, Yan Ni was stopped by Lang Ping, "Yan, you are in the starting lineup tomorrow."

"Eh?" Yan Ni was a little distracted as she was pondering over the key players of the Russian team. Hearing her response, Lang Ping got a bit worried.

"What's the matter? Not ready?" Lang Ping asked.

Standing up straight, Yan Ni hastened to explain that she had got ready.

On the match day, Yan Ni began to feel ill at ease from the moment she got up in the morning, hoping that the match would start as soon as possible. Though she knew such mentality was not helpful to the upcoming competition, she somewhat lost control of herself.

Yan Ni's heart beat extremely fast as she high-fived Lang before the match. This was a feeling she never experienced in the previous nine rounds of the FIVB Volleyball Women's World Cup. She realized it was time for her to play a key role for the team. From the high-five, Yan Ni realized a kind of expectation. It was this moment that helped her further understand the real meaning of the statement: "Long-term training was designed for the real practice."

At the beginning of the match, good preparation led to superior performance of the Chinese team in the first few rallies, and every Chinese player performed smoothly. The girls were concentrated on the match soon, and led with 20-13. The opponent did not give up and spared no efforts to catch up. As a result, the scores were tied at 22-22 and then 23-23. At this critical moment, Zhu Ting showed her prowess. She helped the Chinese team win the first set with an attack and a blocking attempt. With her arms upraised, she joyfully walked around the court for half a circle and high-fived the assistant coach An Jiajie for celebration.

China and Russia won the second and third set respectively. In the fourth set, Russian team had been holding the lead by a small margin until the scores tied at 20-20. Now it was the turn of Yuan Xinyue to serve. She looked for the right place to hit the ball by rolling the ball around in her hands, and then took a deep breath before executing the serve. In this set, Yuan Xinyue executed five serves in a row, and she kept fulfilling the responsibility of serving all the way until the Chinese team won the match. The attack by Zhu Ting, the blocking by Yan Ni and the mistakes made by the opponent under pressure pushed the Chinese team towards the final victory step by step. When it came to the last rally, the Russian player barely received the service by Yuan Xinyue and organized an attack, which was collectively blocked by Liu Yanhan and Yan Ni. The Chinese team won! The team were only one step away from the world champion.

8.

Less than a year later, the Chinese team would once again compete in the final for the world champion title.

After the Chinese team sealed the victory over the Russian team, the Chinese girls knelt on the ground in tears. Lang Ping waited for them at the courtside for a while and then gathered the team together:

Yan Ni is known as the "Great Wall of the North" for her blocking skills. In the competition with the Russian team during the 2015 FIVB Volleyball Women's World Cup, the 28-year-old Yan was entrusted with an important task. (Photo by Li Zhiyan)

"Congratulations to all of you. We won today. Great job! Everyone got involved, and this is our teamwork spirit. But now, it's time for us to calm down and get ready for the next match. I am not too demanding, but the match is not over yet. Our goal has not been achieved since we haven't qualified the Olympic Games. We must stay alert in the crucial competition against the Japanese team tomorrow. So, let's relax ourselves immediately and hurry back to prepare for the upcoming match."

"The competition is not over yet." Lang Ping said so to encourage the Chinese team that had lost to their American counterpart on the third day of the FIVB Volleyball Women's World Cup. At this moment, when the Chinese team were close to the champion title, she still said so.

"I have to say that the Japanese team won't hand over the championship easily. They will surely fight to the last second." Lang Ping repeated before returning to the hotel in the evening to study the match videos of the Japanese team.

It was against the Japanese team in China's last match at the FIVB Volleyball Women's World Cup 34 years ago when Lang Ping made her debut on behalf of the Chinese team. During that match, only by winning two sets could the Chinese team win the championship. It didn't take long before the Chinese team won two sets. After all, it was the first time that they won the world champion. After a short celebration, Lang Ping and her then teammates went on with the match. Although they continued to remind each other that they shouldn't relax, they became so excited that they could not fully concentrate on the match anymore. The Japanese team, on the contrary, with their full devotion, won two sets in a row.

Yuan Weimin, the head coach of the Chinese team at that time, lost his temper, "If you fail to win this match, you'll regret it for the rest of your life!" The above words of Yuan Weimin had been in Lang Ping's memory for 34 years. As she was leading the next-generation women's volleyball players to compete for another FIVB Volleyball Women's World Cup championship, these words occurred to her and brought her mind back to the breathtaking moment when she saw the world championship trophy within touch.

The more critical the moment was, the fewer distractions there should be.

At the preparation meeting, each player hoped to be motivated by other's encouragement. Zhu Ting wrote down on her notebook one of Lang Ping's remarks: "You have to fight for the championship".

However, the very moment Zhu appeared on the court, she felt that the championship title was not far away from her and tried to jump up for it. However, there seemed to be a lot of people below trying to pull her feet down.

9.

This was the final match of the 2015 FIVB Volleyball Women's World Cup.

The Chinese team won the first set 25-17. Then they lost six points consecutively at the mid of the second set. This led to their loss by 22-25 in this set. When the Chinese team lagged behind 8-10 in the crucial third set, Lang Ping requested timeout. Instead of emphasizing too much on technical skills, she just reminded the players to take it easy and relax.

"Am I nervous?" Zhu Ting touched her face subconsciously. Before returning to the playing court, she tried to relax herself by making a smile.

13-16, the Chinese team still lagged behind as they made several mistakes in attack, blocking and defence. The Chinese players furrowed their brows as if saying, "No! How could this happen?" The last step towards victory was supposed to be promising. However, it turned out to be so faltering.

"Hold on! Hold on!" Zeng Chunlei, the captain, clapped her hands and shouted, trying to restore the morale of her teammates and herself.

Over the three years since the team were established, various difficulties happened during daily training. Lang

Ping raised the following requirements for the players: Never give up facing challenges even if they cannot find solutions. During training, sometimes the players didn't perform or co-operate as well as expected. In such cases, Lang Ping always accompanied them without showing her feelings. When the required amount of training had been met, Lang Ping did not end the training by blowing a whistle. Instead, she always accompanied them to go through their physical limit. Then, the players encouraged each other, which led the whole team to a sound state.

After scoring a point with her aggressive attack, Yuan Xinyue stared up at the opponent again. After successfully delivering a back-row attack, Zeng Chunlei smiled again. Then Zeng served an ace, which seemed to make the whole team instantly relaxed. They were not playing well a moment ago, but a little later they were capable of performing whatever actions they wanted. With the persistence of each and every Chinese player in the face of challenge, the Chinese team finally gave full play to their potential!

Then they overtook the opponent 7-1, and then 20-17. The Chinese team not only scored the points, but also regained the fighting spirit as in the competition against the Russian team the day before.

With good serves, the tenacious Japanese team achieved a 20-20 tie. Nevertheless, the Chinese team took the lead in winning the key points at the end of the set, which secured their success in the third set 25-21.

After freeing themselves from psychological shackles, the Chinese team forged ahead for the title.

Leading by 24-21 in the fourth set, the Chinese team now reached the "championship point." Lang Ping substituted Ding Xia with Wei Qiuyue.

This scene moved many fans to tears. They were so excited that they were already on their feet, waiting for the moment when the Chinese team won the world championship for the second time in 11 years. No one had expected that Lang Ping would arrange such a moving scene at the climax of the thrilling competition.

Lang had not made this decision on a whim. After the 2014 FIVB Volleyball Women's World Championship, Wei Qiuyue decided to have an operation in order to compete in the Olympic Games. Over the previous eight months, she had been undergoing difficult postoperative rehabilitation. Witnessing the efforts by this veteran player, Lang Ping fully understood the painful struggle in her heart. She had made this decision when thinking about the personnel deployment before the competition. If circumstances permitted, she would send Wei to the playing court before the end of the match to give Wei a sense of participation that would help boost her confidence.

Standing by the courtside, Wei Qiuyue tried to keep calm, but everyone could read her joy and happiness from her face.

The opponent received the ball served by Wei Qiuyue and delivered a great first-round attack. But Lang Ping insisted on leaving Wei on the court, so that this veteran player could witness the victory on the court. Then the ball went through two rallies between the two teams. Wei passed it to Zhu twice consecutively. For the first time, the Japanese defenders struggled to save the ball. The second time, they tried hard but still watched the ball spiked by Zhu Ting grounded on the playing court.

The Chinese women's volleyball team won this set 25-22! After 11 years, the Chinese team again won the FIVB Volleyball Women's World Cup title after beating Japan 3-1 in 2015!

After scoring the match point, Zhu Ting turned around and pretended to be calm, waiting for the excited teammates who were rushing towards her. Wei Qiuyue, whose injuries prevented her from jumping at full strength during the previous eight months, didn't even realize that she had just jumped so high until she landed on her feet. At this happiest moment, all the Chinese players held together and circled around on the court, cheering heartily.

Lang Ping was interviewed after she won her first world title as the head coach. She had shouted herself hoarse when interviewed. When reviewing the hardships that the Chinese team had gone through during the FIVB Volleyball Women's

The Chinese women's volleyball team took the podium. The jerseys of the players such as Hui Ruoqi and Xu Yunli, who were absent from the competition because of injuries, were very conspicuous. (Photo by Li Zhiyan)

It was so wonderful to win the world championship again after 11 years. The girls of the Chinese women's volleyball team hugged each other after their 3-1 victory over Japan. (Photo by Li Zhiyan)

World Cup, she choked up. "Before whenever I was in trouble, my coach Yuan Weimin encouraged me. He told me that a strong person is born out of challenges."

CHAPTER FOUR

2016

The Chinese team never give up fighting

2016 was China's Lunar Year of the Monkey.

"It's the Chinese zodiac year in which Langlang (Nickname of Bai Lang) was born. My daughter is 24." Lang Ping sighed deeply at the thought.

How time flied! Bai Lang, daughter of Lang Ping, was in many people's memory still a four-year-old girl who sat on her mother's lap to cheer on the Chinese women's volleyball team at the 1996 Atlanta Olympic Games, and the 16-year-old high school student would return to China with her mother for the 2008 Beijing Olympic Games.

At that moment, Bai was on a flight from San Francisco to Beijing to attend her mother's wedding.

After she came of age, she had been hoping that her mother would get remarried. She felt painful at the thought of her mother living alone for so many years.

On January 16, 2016, Bai Lang appeared in her mother's wedding ceremony. Holding the wedding ring of her mother, she walked slowly to the stage and offered her love and blessing.

Five days later, Lang Ping happily resumed her work in preparation for the ultimate challenge of the 2016 Rio Olympic Games.

1.

With the women's volleyball training hall lighted up, the Chinese women's volleyball team for the Olympic Games came together.

"The world championship is not our ultimate goal. Instead, it marks a new beginning for us." As Lang Ping spoke, her eyes fell on a dark-skinned girl in the middle of the second row. This girl, dressed in a bright blue long-sleeved training suit, was conspicuous against a group of players in pale yellow short-sleeved T-shirts. The girl was Gong Xiangyu. Born on April 21, 1997, she was the setter of the National Junior Team in the spring of 2013. It was less than half a year after she was recruited into the provincial team of Jiangsu Province. With the arrival of Gong, Yuan Xinyue was no longer the "youngest team player." As the teammates in the National Junior Team, Gong and Yuan never expected that less than three years later they would become teammates again in the national team.

On February 12, just after the Spring Festival of the Year of the Monkey, the Chinese team began their preparations for the 2016 Rio Olympic Games.

It was a day of special commemorative significance for Lang Ping and the Chinese team. On February 12, 1995, Lang Ping, at the age of 34, was appointed as the head coach of the Chinese team by China's State Sports Commission.

Lang Ping, twice entrusted with such an important mission at critical moments, led the underperforming Chinese team to get out of trouble. Lang Ping made her legends with continuous efforts. As a result, she ranked among the top 10 figures of Touching China 2015. The citation of Touching China 2015 for Lang Ping aroused nation-wide resonance.

"In the face of adversity, Lang Ping led a soul-stirring competition against strong rivals despite challenges, setbacks and pains. The Chinese team fully demonstrated the spirit of struggle. Generations of athletes have practiced so hard in recovering balls, jumping and spiking. These efforts really help awaken China's aspiration for becoming stronger. The 'Iron Hammer', born to play volleyball and play for honor, has become a legend!"

The "Iron Hammer" legend represents the legend of the Chinese team. Lang Ping embodies the values of the Chinese people: continuous self-renewal, no fear of difficulties and self-motivation.

2.

The top priority for the Chinese women's volleyball team during the winter training for the Olympic Games was to conquer the Brazilian team.

"We have won the world championship, but we haven't beaten the Brazilian team and the U.S. team!" Before the winter training camp began, Lang Ping said, "If we aim for a medal, we can't avoid meeting the two teams and we will inevitably encounter one of them in the semi-final."

The Rio Olympic Games was the fourth one that Lang Ping took part in.

"Different from the FIVB Volleyball Women's World Championship and the FIVB Volleyball Women's World Cup, during the Olympic Games the knockout stage will begin once the eight-team finals are determined. Losers in the following quarter-finals and semi-finals will be knocked out directly. Only by making a breakthrough can we continue to fight in the following matches." The priority will be on how to outplay Brazil, a strong opponent to whom China had lost 18 matches in a row over eight years.

The first month of the winter training was called the "Brazilian Month." Just as the name suggested, this month focused on practicing how to deal with the Brazilian team.

It had been Lang Ping's long-term habit to prepare for everything in advance. An Jiajie and she had made the schedule for the "Brazilian Month" before the training camp. Various issues ranging from monthly objectives to the arrangement of each training session had been discussed about in detail. Lang even asked her friends working in Brazil to help rent a training court for the Chinese team in Rio during the Olympic Games.

When it came to training, Lang Ping tried to carry out each training item in strict accordance with the strengths of the Brazilian team, such as the defence training, the timing of coaches' actions and the command of ball speed.

3.

This was the first time that the Chinese women's volleyball team selected 12 from 22 players in their history. They had to face the tough choice three months before the start of the Olympic Games.

Lang Ping hoped that more players would be available for each position.

From the first day since she took charge of the Chinese team in 2013, she has spared no efforts to develop a "Big

National Team." In the first year, the team had to be established in haste since time was limited. As information came from various sources, she assembled a 23-person roster consisting of both veteran players and new recruits.

In 2014 she decided to further enhance such efforts, formulating a training list of 27-member, the largest ever national team. In 2015 and 2016, the national team remained the size of 26 players.

In the FIVB World Grand Prix two months before the Olympic Games, the Chinese team submitted a list of 21 players. All the 20 players chosen for the final-stage preparation for the Olympic Game competed on the court. All key players including Zhu Ting must improve their skills through training and real competitions. Although the time available for each Chinese player varied, everyone had chance to prove herself.

There was no best individual, but there could be a best group.

Lang Ping often tells her players that volleyball shows the charm of teamwork.

"The 12 players for the 2016 Rio Olympic Games shouldn't just feel they were lucky dogs. Instead, they should realize they shoulder the mission and responsibility of the whole team in the Olympic Games."

The choice of the last candidate for the 12-member list had to be made between Zeng Chunlei and Gong Xiangyu, both opposites of similar technical features, respectively from the old and young generation of players. Lang Ping was lost in thought as for who was the right candidate for helping the Chinese team perform better in the upcoming competition.

Zeng, the captain of the Chinese team winning the World

Cup championship, who once accepted the mission of leading the team during the most difficult times, has been underperforming over the previous one year; Gong, a newbie, despite her lack of world-class competition experience, has been making astonishing progress over the previous half a year after joining the national team.

Before making the final decision, the coaches and leaders held two meetings. It turned out that three members of the FIVB Volleyball Women's World Cup championship team were denied the access to the Olympic Games, including Zeng Chunlei, Shen Jingsi and Wang Mengjie.

Gong Xiangyu, who had been a member of the Chinese team for just five months, was "shocked" when learning that she was among the 12 players for the Olympic Games. Both her coaches and teammates could feel that this young girl freaked out under pressure and was trying to conceal her inner tension.

"When I was 18 years old, Coach Yuan Weimin improved my ability by sending me to compete in the Asian Women's Volleyball Championship, during which my performance was not as good as expected. However, I performed much better during the following Olympic Games." At this critical moment, Lang Ping remembered the choice made by Yuan Weimin, her coach.

During the 1978 Asian Games, Yuan Weimin, despite different views, insisted on replacing Yang Xi, a veteran who was still at her peak, with Lang Ping who just joined the national team. Lang Ping started the first set against South Korea with power attacks. However, she made frequent mistakes and was substituted in the second set against Japan. Yuan Weimin didn't change his mind. He decided to break the convention by using promising new recruiters even at certain cost. He proved to be right. By the 1981 FIVB Volleyball Women's

World Cup, the 21-year-old Lang Ping had become the key player of the team.

At this point, Lang Ping was quite concerned about the schedule of Wang Mengjie, the last one to leave the team. She told Lai Yawen that the girl should better not stay until the day to see off her teammates. "She stays here so late for offering support for our training. She will be left alone after we're gone. Please ask Mengjie to go home after our last training session was over."

Unexpectedly, Wang Mengjie changed her flight as soon as she received the ticket booking information, because she wanted to see the team off together with Zeng Chunlei and Shen Jingsi who came all the way from their homes. Although this would make her feel sicker at heart, she still wanted to stay a little longer with her coaches including Lang Ping and her teammates, as she hated to part with this team.

4.

The Olympic Games was a new starting point.

Of the Chinese team for the Rio Olympic Games, nine players took part in the Olympic Games for the first time. Only through one's personal experience with such event could she fully understand the fierce competition of the world-class matches. Lang Ping believed that veteran players like Xu Yunli would play a special role at critical moments.

One year ago, standing beside the bus, Xu Yunli saw off her teammates. This time, with full confidence, she embarked on her third Olympic journey. Encouraged by Lang Ping at this crucial moment, Xu Yunli knew that as the oldest player of the team, she needed to take on more responsibilities during the Olympic Games and tried to share more workload of the coaches.

"Coach Lang, thanks for your trust all the time. Your encouragement has enabled me to persist until now with strong motivation. Since this opportunity does not come easily, I will cherish it even more and will do my best to fight for the dream with my teammates!"

This was Xu Yunli's reply to Lang Ping after deliberation.

Usually, it wouldn't take her a long time to reply to Lang Ping with a message. However, this time she felt something different because she had a premonition that the Chinese team might not go on as smoothly as expected during the 2016 Rio Olympic Games and would even encounter some challenges.

Departing from Beijing, the Chinese team, after transfer in Frankfurt, arrived in Sao Paulo first, where they stayed for two days. Then they flew to Rio de Janeiro. After over 30 hours of flight, the Chinese team arrived at the Southern Hemisphere of the world. There was a 11-hour time difference between Beijing in summer and Rio in winter. It was a really weird feeling for the Chinese team.

In the first match, the Chinese team competed against the Netherlands team, a European top team that performed quite well in the year of Olympic Games. With 14-13 in the deciding set, the Dutch team got the match point. Even at that time, still few people believed that the Chinese team would lose this match. With a power attack, Lonneke Sloetjes scored the match point. This led to the victory of the Dutch team with 15-13. In this match, Sloetjes scored a total of 26 points, two points more than that of Zhu Ting, the "Best Scorer" of the Chinese team.

The Chinese team held a meeting in the evening to find

out the problems. In Lang Ping's words, it didn't matter if we lost a match, and what really mattered was that we must know why we lost and what our weaknesses were. The players enumerated many similar cases. For example, the Chinese players felt that the balls spiked by the opponents were at rather high speed. However, they felt the ball spiked by themselves couldn't reach that speed. They would be extremely excited whenever they succeeded in spiking a ball, while they would be discouraged if they didn't perform well enough in spiking.

Lang Ping made a good summary: "The opponents are eager to win, while we believe that we should win. During the match, we would complain when something went wrong. On the contrary, the opponents weren't distracted by such matter. Instead, they were determined to wage a fierce battle!"

The Chinese team wouldn't get through the group stage unless they no longer made low-level mistakes during the following two matches with Italy and Puerto Rico. However, there remained little chance for the Chinese team to obtain a good team ranking. After the first match, the Chinese team were destined to go through many challenges during the Rio Olympic Games.

5.

From the first day after arrival in Rio, Gong Xiangyu couldn't sleep well every night.

Previously, whenever she went to bed, she could fall asleep at once. After she entered the Olympic Village, under the heavy pressure, there seemed a movie playing in her head as soon as she went to bed. She couldn't help thinking something over. Hours had passed until she felt sleepy, but it was already dawn before she slept tight. Nevertheless, she had to pluck up courage to get up for training in the morning.

The pressure was so great for this young girl who took part in such a world-class event for the first time, that she was psychologically overwhelmed. She couldn't hold back her tears at the thought of the match.

Gong Xiangyu, a sensible girl, knew that the coaches were quite busy during the Olympic Games. She felt more uneasy as two coaches were taking care of her. On one occasion, An Jiajie talked with her and she couldn't help crying again: "Coach An, I feel sorry for you and my teammates. It was I that hindered our whole team and you really shouldn't have brought me here."

Hearing her words, Coach An didn't know how to respond. He said: "Xiangyu, we decided to bring you here because we believe in your potential. In the case of your good performance, it is your achievement; in the case of your poor performance, the coach team take the blame!" An Jiajie tried his best to help her cope with stress.

However, it was the words of Lang Ping that really alleviated her stress.

One night after dinner, Lang saw Gong at the Olympic Village canteen and called her to come over. Before stopping in front of Lang Ping, Gong couldn't refrain her tears from flowing down.

"I was told that you thought I shouldn't have selected you into the team. Did you say that?" Gong Xiangyu was somewhat surprised by Lang Ping's words.

She nodded silently and continued wiping away her tears.

"What can I do now?" Lang Ping sounded as if she was coaxing a child or discussing a solution with her.

Unexpectedly, this really helped Gong Xiangyu follow Lang Ping's train of thought and stopped crying. Lang Ping continued, "Shall I bring you back to China? And find a substitute for you? It's too late since the match has begun and it's so far away from China."

Gong couldn't help smiling at Lang Ping's embarrassed expression. Of course, she knew it was impossible.

Lang Ping took advantage of this good opportunity: "So don't doubt your abilities anymore. I have no substitute for you."

In addition to Gong Xiangyu, Ding Xia, who won the world title a year ago, also could hardly withstand the pressure brought by the Olympic Games.

An Jiajie and Lai Yawen helped her to reduce psychological burden with great efforts. However, Ding began to doubt her abilities again after failing to cooperate well with the spiker: "Am I qualified? Shouldn't the coach have brought me here?" Ding also thought it shouldn't be this case. She even talked to herself: "Aren't you quite confident? How can you doubt yourself? What a loser!"

The match against the Italian team was the decisive competition for the Chinese team to pass the group stage. Before the match, Lang Ping called Zhu Ting aside and said, "This is a critical competition. You must stand up to it!"

Lang Ping did not dare to say so in front of the whole team. As a veteran with rich competition experience, she knew she should use various approaches to mobilize players of different personalities at such a critical moment.

In fact, the match against the Italian team was relatively smooth. The Chinese team enjoyed advantage throughout the whole match. However, as the match result would determine if the Chinese team could pass the group stage, the Chinese players failed to perform as well as expected under such great pressure.

China lost to Serbia 0-3 in the fourth round of the group stage. Even at the end of the match, the Chinese players still couldn't accept the reality. Why all the efforts of the previous day turned out to be in vain during the match? The loss of the first match was attributed to nervousness. However, why such condition didn't get improved until the fourth match. Why no obvious progress could be achieved as expected after so many meetings and discussions?

With two wins and two losses, China failed to meet the expected target. If the competition between Serbia and the Netherlands could go into a fifth set and the Netherlands finally won, China would just rank the fourth even if they could upset the U.S. team later.

According to the match rules, the team ranking the fourth place in one group would compete with the team of the first place of another group when the quarterfinals began. In this case, the Chinese team were most likely to challenge the host Brazilian team. Over the previous eight years, except the victory over Brazil in the Macau competition of the FIVB Volleyball Women's World Championship, China had lost 18 times in a row to Brazil. In this case, the following competition for China would be incredibly challenging.

That night, Yuan Xinyue lost sleep. Throughout the four matches that the Chinese team had completed in the 2016 Rio Olympic Games, the team were in a difficult situation. Each time when Yuan Xinyue played on the court, whether as a starting player or substitute, she hoped that she could serve as an unexpected sunday punch, just as she did during the 2014 FIVB Volleyball Women's World Championship and the 2015 FIVB Volleyball Women's World Cup. However, such magic power didn't come as she expected.

Zhu Ting, a pretty sound sleeper, also stared at the ceiling for a long time. She was puzzled as to what on earth was the pressure of the Olympic Games? Finding that Xu Yunli also did not fall asleep, Zhu Ting chatted with her.

In the next room, Zhang Changning was also talking with Ding Xia, "My parents set off today. They plan to watch our matches from the quarterfinals. As they take a long trip here, I really can't bear to see that they can only watch one match before they return to China."

In another room, Hui Ruoqi and Lin Li were also having a "bedtime chat". "I am feeling very sad. As the captain of the team, I failed to fulfil my role during the previous matches," said Hui Ruoqi, who could not help revealing what she had kept in her heart for days. "Sister Hui. This isn't the case. I feel very at ease as long as you stand beside me on the court!" replied Lin Li. Lin Li just told the truth. However, upon hearing such words, Hui Ruoqi said in a choked voice: "Li, I must live up to your expectation. I will try my best to become vigorous again. Fight!"

During the next day of training session, Lang refused the visits by anyone. She would like to take this opportunity to guide the girls to "mediate on the meaning of life."

6.

There was just 50 hours left for the Chinese team in Rio Olympic Games.

The Chinese team ranked the fourth in their group after losing 1-3 to the U.S. team, their long-term opponent. This meant that the Chinese team had to defeat the Brazilian team, the host country team in the quarterfinals two days later, otherwise they would be eliminated.

It is said that team sports require even higher skills and better cooperation, because all the team players need to make concerted efforts to achieve their common goal. This isn't hard to do when the match was played in a smooth manner. However, the real test for team sports comes when faced with difficulties.

In this case of the Chinese players at the time, every player had her own idea. She might worry about herself, suspect her teammates, fear the difficulty, feel oppressed or be in a bad temper. Even worse, no one was willing to share her real ideas voluntarily.

It was almost an impossible task for the coaches to find out and understand the problems and come up with solutions within so limited time. However, they still believed that it was worth the efforts.

When Lang Ping talked to Yan Ni, this stubborn girl was still wondering how she could get over the difficulty.

"Ni, are you still feeling depressed?" Upon hearing Lang Ping's words, Yan Ni couldn't help crying.

"Coach Lang, I feel guilty." Yan Ni wiped her tears after saying these words. Her response was no surprise for Lang Ping. However, Lang was somewhat surprised by Yan's response.

On hearing this, Lang Ping understood that the kindhearted Yan Ni loved her very much. To her shame, Lang Ping, under such a heavy burden and great pressure, had to bother to cheer her up. However, she, the second oldest player of the team, didn't offer help as needed to the coaches.

"Ni, all our team players for the Rio Olympic Games are the best ones. We as coaches trust you and quite understand how you feel now. However, our long-term efforts aim to achieve our common goal. Although we have lost the three previous matches, we still have one last chance. So now we need to calm down and focus on performing well in the last match. Whatever happens in the end, let's try not to leave ourselves with any regrets…"

Upon hearing these words, Yan Ni felt that she suddenly extricated herself from many previous complicated emotions. As she came to realize the following match would be their final opportunity in the Rio Olympic Games, what had puzzled her suddenly became something of less concern for her.

"Xiao Li, tomorrow when practicing playing actions, I will try to make improvement. Please stand beside me to give me some advices! Just tell me, if any, and I'll make adjustment!" Just before going to bed in the evening, Xu Yunli received this message from Yan Ni. This was really good news for Xu Yunli as it indicated that Yan Ni ultimately figured it out!

On the way to the training venue early in the morning of the 15th of August, Lang Ping saw Cristo Redentor, the most recognizable symbol of Rio, in the distance. She whispered to Lai Yawen: "If today we lose the match to the Brazilian team, shall we take our players to pay a visit there? They have come all this way here but still don't even know what Rio is like!"

Lai Yawen frowned: "If it were in that case, that means we even don't rank among the final four. I think we should just go home." As the "housekeeper" of the team, Lai Yawen had to make various arrangements for the whole team every time she led the team to attend competitions. If the Chinese team lost in the match against the Brazilian team, they would be eliminated. Therefore, she began checking the return tickets from the previous evening, but no enough tickets were available for the whole team in any flight to China in the following few days. She also worried about the 30 volleyballs brought from Beijing. All of them had to be taken away from the training court after the training session in the morning ended in the match day.

"Shall we deflate those balls?" She whispered to Lang Ping.

Lang Ping, apparently having not thought about that question, did not answer it right away.

"We just brought an inflator with us. If we defeat the Brazilian team, we have to pump up all balls, which will be a big problem."

Lai Yawen had taken everything into account.

If the Chinese team couldn't win the following competition against Brazil, it would be the last 24 hours for the Chinese team at the Rio Olympic Games.

7.

After dinner, Lang Ping and Lai Yawen held a meeting with the players. After the meeting, Xu Yunli, Wei Qiuyue and Hui Ruoqi were left. As all of them were senior members, the two coaches asked them to further communicate with their teammates, so as to learn what their concerns were. The coaches worried that their direct communication with players by themselves at this time might impose too much pressure on them.

After consultation with her roommate Zhu Ting, Xu Yunli proposed to have a group discussion with Zhang Changning and Ding Xia who lived in the same unit. She did so because she worried that there wouldn't be enough time for one-to-one communication.

Under such specific circumstances and at this special moment, Xu Yunli, through her frank opening remarks, struck a chord with Zhu Ting, Zhang Changning and Ding Xia.

Being outspoken and straightforward, Ding Xia preferred to communicate in this manner: "Li, in the fifth set of our first match against the Netherlands, you committed a serving fault. I would like to make a suggestion. As a veteran player, you'd better not miss your service in such a crucial match."

Respecting senior members is a tradition in China's sports community. In normal conditions, Ding Xia would never say so. Her frankness was beyond Xu Yunli's expectations, which even made the veteran player feel embarrassed.

"Yes, I shouldn't have made such a mistake. I will try to do well in the following match." Xu Yunli felt her heart pounding as she made the above self-criticism.

With their hearts wide open, they put all their worries aside and determined to seize the opportunity for preventing the Chinese team from being knocked out. Such life experience would be unique for anyone. The chatting was drawing their hearts closer: "We have gone through various hardships before coming to the 2016 Rio Olympic Games. We are now in very difficult situation in spite of our four-year great efforts. We must support each other to go through the hard times."

The four girls talked until two o'clock in the morning. After Zhang Changning and Ding Xia went back to their room, Zhu Ting was lying in bed tossing and turning, chatting with Xu Yunli almost till dawn.

The match was scheduled to start at 10:30 p.m. local

time, so there was still time for training in the morning. It would be the last training session of the Chinese team in the Rio Olympic cycle if they lost this match in the evening.

"This should be my last training session with them. I will stick to the end!"

On the way to the training session, Lang Ping sent this text message to her friend. This indicated that she prepared for the hardest match.

Lang Ping had told Lai Yawen how to deflate the volleyballs: "Deflate half of them. Please make sure that Wu Xiaolei and Li Tong do that after training, so that the players won't see this."

8.

Back to the Olympic Village, Zhu Ting was ready to have a good sleep after lunch to prepare for the "crucially important competition" in the evening. After communication with coaches and teammates, Zhu Ting felt her mood had become much more relaxed and cheerful. However, as outside hitter and best scorer of the team, Zhu still felt a lot of pressure, as if her chest were being pressed by something.

After the training session in the morning, Lang Ping was chatting with Li Tong and Doctor Hou at the entrance of the training venue. She saw Zhu Ting coming out first after bathing and wanted to invite her to go to the backyard together to see monkeys. Unexpectedly, Zhu Ting directly got into the bus and said dully, "Excuse me, Coach Lang, I want to have a rest."

At the 1984 Los Angeles Olympic Games, Lang Ping, then 24, was the key to the team's success or failure. In the first round, she underperformed as she was restricted by her opponents. China lost to their American counterpart in this match. Later, the two teams met again in the final competition for the championship. Lang Ping must perform quite well, otherwise the Chinese team were unlikely to win the "triple crown."

In this crucially important competition, Zhu Ting, the leading scorer of the Chinese team, was under enormous pressure. It was only Lang Ping who could understand such pressure and know how to best unleash the great potential of this talented spiker.

"Zhu Ting, it was predestined that I became your coach. Among the numerous players that I have coached around the world, you are the best one I am most proud of. For the upcoming competition, I believe in you and you must believe in yourself, too. You are the best player on the playing court! Any challenge will prove to be a test for you. I believe you will be able to overcome any difficulty! Fight!"

Zhu Ting, who was about to take a nap, cried inside the quilt after reading the message from Lang Ping.

Shedding tears was really a good means for Zhu Ting to reduce psychological stress before such an important match.

Zhu Ting always raised extremely high requirements for herself. However, from the beginning of the World Grand Prix before the Olympic Games, she found no matter how she tried, she couldn't perform well as expected. This was exerting increasing pressure on her. She tried every means to make adjustment but failed.

Receiving recognition from Coach Lang at such critical moment, Zhu Ting was very excited. This allowed her to relieve her pressure with her tears.

Zhu Ting tried to calm herself down. Then, after deliberation for a while, she replied to Lang Ping.

"Coach Lang, thank you very much. You are so nice to me. I am honored to be your team player. I will spare no efforts for scoring every point."

A preparation meeting was held in the afternoon.

"Today's match may be the last one for us together. Every point during the match may involve your offering protection to your teammates or your last pass in this match. So, I hope everyone present on the court should cherish every point and fully unleash her potential. As long as the ball hasn't been grounded on the playing court, there is still hope." The words by Hui Ruoqi moved many people present into tears.

Finally, Lang Ping motivated the players with her own success stories, which made all players very excited.

Beginning with the fact that the "old-generation Chinese team" won the first three world champion titles all by outplaying the host country teams, Lang Ping told the Chinese players that the host country teams were not as powerful as they thought. The Chinese players of this team also had similar experience in this aspect. For example, in both the semi-finals of the 2014 FIVB Volleyball Women's World Championship and the final round of the 2015 FIVB Volleyball Women's World Cup, the Chinese team all won the host country teams.

"Brazilian team are really very strong. However, whatever the result is, they shall never expect easy victory over us! They must underestimate we Chinese team. So, as long as we exert excessive pressure on them, they will inevitably panic and shake their confidence. It never occurs to them that they will be denied the access to the final four. Their only goal is to win the championship."

"The fans cheering for the Brazilian team will be seen everywhere in the stadium. Don't feel depressed. How many fans do we Chinese team have? It is no exaggeration to say there are at least more than one hundred million. With so many supporters behind us, we are not lonely."

At 7:15 p.m., the Chinese team left the Olympic Village for the competition venue.

9.

The competition was held at Ginasio do Maracanazinho in Rio on August 16.

The quarterfinal between the Chinese and Brazilian Women's Volleyball Teams began at 10:30 p.m. local time. It happened to be the time for Brazilians to enjoy themselves by drinking and chatting. Having not dropped a single set until their quarter-final shocker against China, the Brazilian team had won five matches in a row without losing a set or even feeling nervous about the pressure by the opponents' competition. Such easy and happy victories made every night's carnival after the Brazilian's victory more enjoyable than ever.

Perhaps to the excited Brazilian fans, the Chinese team couldn't pose any threat to the Brazilian team that aimed for a third consecutive Olympic title because the Chinese team underperformed and seldom won their Brazilian counterpart for years. The fans underestimated the Chinese team so much that when the two teams appeared on the court, some local fans even shouted in English: "Go home! Go home!"

From the performance of the two teams in the first set, it was likely that the Chinese team would soon lose the competition.

From the beginning of the first set, the Brazilian team had been keeping ahead. One Brazilian player even rushed to the bumper plate at the end line to fulfill her defence. "Their defence is really good," Lang Ping said with a smile to Lai Yawen. "Our team were still somewhat inferior. I won't regret even if we lose this match!"

Brazil won the first set with 25-15, their victory for the 16th set in a row since the start of the Olympic Games.

Despite such an unfavorable situation with scores far behind the opponent, Lang Ping still kept watching the rhythm of each player on the court, preparing for shifts and substitutions in the second set.

When the Brazilian team led the second set with 21-18, the Brazilian coach Guimaraes saw Lang Ping requesting substitution. However, he didn't pay much attention to the No.10 player Liu Xiaotong who just appeared on the court after the substitution. Before the Olympic Games began, Brazil invited China for a match of five sets. Brazil won all the first four sets. He even ignored the fact that it was Liu Xiaotong, who as a substitute, helped the Chinese team win the 5th set.

In her preparation for this crucially important match with the Brazilian team, Lang Ping had assigned Liu Xiaotong with the role as a super-sub. If the starting lineup failed to gain the upper hand, she planned to bring Liu Xiaotong on to exert more pressure on the opponent. During the training before the match, Lang Ping told Liu Xiaotong to get fully prepared for playing on the court upon her order. At such a critical moment that the Chinese team lagged behind with 18-21, they must hold off the opponent, otherwise the Brazilian team would soon win the second set. Lang Ping waved to Liu Xiaotong on the bench: "It's your turn!"

Liu Xiaotong faced a test as soon as she went onto the court. During the counterattack, when Zhu Ting shifted the ball to the zone 4, Liu Xiaotong jumped and saw the defence by the opponent's middle blocker Thaisa Daher De Menezes and the setter Danielle Lins, who were both very high. She made the attack cleverly. The ball was spiked off the blocking and grounded on the back zone of the Brazilian court. The Brazilian defenders failed to save it and the Chinese team scored a point!

After fulfilling this wonderful attack at this critical moment, Liu Xiaotong rotated to the back row. Her previous attack not only fully enhanced her confidence, but also greatly encouraged her teammates. For the last few points of the second set, the Brazilian team still competed rather fiercely. But the Chinese team had found the right rhythm. After a 23-23 tie, when it was the turn of Liu Xiaotong to serve, Zhu scored a point with a power attack. Then she successfully blocked the spike by Sheilla Castro De Paula Blassioli, one of the key players of the Brazilian team.

The Chinese team managed to turn the table in the second set and the Brazilian team lost this set, the first set they lost after the beginning of the Olympic Games. Then the two sides changed sides and went on with the competition. Though it seemed that nothing had changed on the surface, in fact certain psychological changes had already taken place.

All the Chinese players smiled happily when Zhu Ting scored the first point of the third set by digging the ball into the Brazilian team's back zone. Just as Lang Ping had analyzed for them before this match, the Brazilian players would make mistakes if the pressure was too heavy for them. It was not a good thing for the Brazilian team that their previous competitions since the beginning of the Olympic Games went on so smoothly.

In the previous two sets, the ball spiked by the Brazilian players could always be grounded on the court of the Chinese team as they expected. Seeing the Chinese players being incapable of blocking or defending their attacks, the Brazilian players roared with laughter while waving their fists. However, this was completely changed. The Chinese players could always defend and save the ball skillfully. The libero Lin Li, in particular, no longer performed as clumsily as she did in the previous matches. Instead, in this match she was quick in reaction and light-footed. She seemed so capable of anticipating where the ball would ground that she could always appear in the most appropriate place in advance. She said to herself: "We must not give up. I don't want our team to be eliminated!"

Zhang Changning performed quite well that day. She came onto the court as a substitute in the first set and occupied a starting position in second one. It was really remarkable that she successfully handled serve receiving and achieved high accuracy of serve receiving. Before entering the court, she was looking towards the cheering crowds carrying five-star red flags to search for her parents who came from afar. She said that since childhood she never lost in the matches at which her parents were present. Was Zhang really endowed with the magic power from her family?

The Chinese team outplayed their opponent with 25-22 in the third set. They surpassed the Brazilian team with 2-1. This allowed the Chinese players to find the hope of success.

For the first point of the fourth set, Liu Xiaotong of the Chinese team demonstrated wonderful skills in defence, which was as capable as that by the Brazilian counterpart in saving the ball near the bumper plate at the end line in the first set. After Liu Xiaotong received the ball while running, Zhu Ting scored a point with a spike. As a result, the Brazilian players were stunned.

China led with 8-7 when switching side in deciding set.

When the Brazilian team lagged behind with 10-12, the grandson of the Brazilian coach Guimaraes already felt helpless with eyes swelling with tears.

At this point, Jaqueline Pereira De Carvalho Endres, a veteran player who had participated in the Olympic Games for three times, stood on the bench of the Brazilian team, with her hands covering her forehead and not daring to watch the match. The Brazilian team members were becoming increasingly impatient.

The score was 14-13. This meant that the Chinese team would win the match if they could score one more point. At this critical moment, Lang Ping requested timeout.

After discussing with Wei Qiuyue on how to handle the last point, Lang Ping turned to Zhu Ting with a wink and said, "Zhu, prepare for back-row attack!" Zhu found that Wei was also looking at her. They said nothing to each other but stared at each other until they entered the match again and the referee blew the whistle indicating that it was time for the Brazilian team to serve.

After the ball was served by the opponent, Zhang Changning offered a good serve receiving and Xu Yunli moved behind Wei Qiuyue and pretended to carry a quick attack. This action attracted Natalia Pereira away from her position. When Natalia realized she was misguided and tried to return to block the spike by Zhu Ting, the ball passed by Wei Qiuyue was already spiked by Zhu Ting who jumped high behind the 3-meter line. The ball went out of bounds after hitting the fingertips of Natalia. The Chinese team won!

With 3-2, the Chinese team eliminated Brazil and went into the quarterfinals!

Zhu lost in thought for two seconds when she scored the winning point. Even after celebrating for the victory together with her teammates, she still could hardly believe it was true. It was so fantastic. She didn't expect that with concerted efforts, the Chinese team could overcome so great a challenge and upset this powerful opponent.

Zhang Changning, who performed quite well throughout the match, couldn't help crying when hugging Zhu Ting, Xu Yunli and Ding Xia. After the event, she suddenly felt somewhat panicky at the idea that the result might be different if the Chinese team had made more mistakes during such a fierce competition.

The four girls thought of what they were chatting last night, and their group photo taken at the gate of their room before setting off from the Olympic Village for the competition. They also wondered why they felt lonely and helpless themselves but felt they were so powerful when working together!

After hugging her coaches and teammates, Wei Qiuyue took a look at the Brazilian players on the other side of the court. Sheilla was crying, Fabiana Claudino was crying, and Jaqueline, with her face wet with tears, hugged her teammates and comforted each other.

Only then did Lai Yawen say to Lang Ping: "Last night, I had a dream." In her dream, the Chinese team won the match. However, when walking out of the gym after the press conference, she found the bus for the team had left. "We ultimately got a big motorcycle. We put on big helmets and rode back to the Olympic Village." Lai Yawen talked about her dream with gestures.

It was a beautiful night for the Chinese team in Rio.

10.

When the training session ended at the previous night, Lai Yawen left Li Tong and Wu Xiaolei to deflate half of the volleyballs. Asked what he would do if the Chinese team won the match against Brazil, Li said: "If we win, I will be willing to inflate these balls with my mouth!"

On August 17, it was already after 2:00 a.m. when Wu Xiaolei and Li Tong returned from the competition venue to their apartment that was outside the Olympic village. They woke up in the early morning before the alarm clock rang. After washing up, they went to bed but didn't fall asleep immediately. Both of them were thinking about the volleyballs which had been deflated.

In order not to delay the team's training, they set off an hour earlier than usual, trying to get all the volleyballs ready before the players arrived.

The moment he pushed open the door of the training hall, the assistant coach Wu Xiaolei felt that he became energetic again. After all, when he left here the day before, he said to himself: "I hope that we can return here tomorrow to go on with training."

Only a small inflator was available for so many volleyballs in the trolley. It soon became so hot only after pumping the ball up for less than one minute. They had to wait for it to become cool before going on pumping up.

After the Chinese players arrived and lined up, Lang Ping began her instruction in a playful manner.

"I told you yesterday that it was our last training session here. You all couldn't accept it and insisted on going on with training here. To this end, you gave full play to your potential and ultimately tried your best to win the match. Of course, I know that you are shrewd in money matters and know Coach Lai's reservation of the training hall won't expire until August 20. Aware that our payment won't be refunded if we leave in advance, you want to have more drills here so that our cost of renting the gym is worthwhile, right?"

Her words started us all off laughing.

But she quickly moved to reminding the players that among the final four teams, the Chinese team ranked the fourth. The Netherlands, Serbia and the U.S. had all upset China in the group stage. She added that the Chinese players had to start from scratch again and devote themselves to making a breakthrough!

The girls lined up and began running exercise. Lang Ping made stretching exercises at the courtside. The assistant coaches took this time to do physical exercises, and the fitness trainer Rett was preparing the warm-up equipment.

Every Chinese team member cherished the chance to stay on the playing court after going through so great a challenge.

Lang Ping led the players to practice digging drills in groups. In the previous day, Zhu Ting scored points through her digging actions during the competition with the Brazilian team that excelled in technical skills. Before beginning the drills, Lang Ping proposed that everyone applaud Zhu Ting for her good performance. During the training break, someone mentioned the Olympic Village, a topic that soon aroused a heated discussion among these girls: "More than ten days have passed, but we seldom have a careful look at the Olympic Village. Fortunately, we won Brazil, otherwise we really don't have the opportunity to see what the Olympic Village really looks like."

Before the semi-final between China and the Netherlands, the United States and Serbia would play first in the other half. Unexpectedly, after five-set fierce competition, Serbia upset the United States that ranked the first place in the world and were among the most favorites for the title. This was really major good news for the Chinese team as they had lost most of the competitions against their American counterpart during the Rio Olympic cycle. Of course, to meet the Serbian team in the final, the Chinese team must outplay the Dutch team first.

At the pre-match meeting in preparation for the competition between China and the Netherlands, Lang Ping asked everyone to try their best to defeat the opponent.

Before setting off for the competition, Zhu Ting, Xu Yunli, Ding Xia and Zhang Changning had an "oath-taking" ceremony in the living room—The four girls shouted simultaneously: "Come on tonight! Fight!"

Zhang Changning made another request: "Sister Li, if we win today, could you please make noodles for us as a reward please?"

In the first set, when the Chinese team led with 24-21, the Netherlands tried to equalize the score. It was the continuous power attack by Zhu Ting that helped the Chinese team win this set with 27-25.

In the second set, the Netherlands found an effective way to defend Zhu. As a result, Zhu had to make more efforts for every point she scored. At the end of this set, the

Netherlands' coach Giovanni Guidetti sent the substitute Celeste Plak who had posed great challenges to China in the opening match of the Olympic Games. His tactics proved to be quite effective, which helped the Netherlands win the second set with 25-23.

After two sets, Zhu Ting had already scored 20 points. It became a common concern as to whether her physical strength could sustain under such fierce competition. When the Chinese team lagged behind by 0-6 at the beginning of the third set, the Chinese side felt really worried.

When the Chinese team fell behind with 2-8, the Chinese team requested substitution. The Chinese player that entered the match was Gong Xiangyu, who once could not help crying after China lost to the Netherlands at the group stage.

Of the 12 Chinese players, Gong was the only one that didn't play in the quarter-final against Brazil. Gong Xiangyu, perhaps moved by the passion of her teammates in this critical competition, said to the setter Ding Xia: "If Coach Lang sends me onto the court, please pass me the ball. I am confident in delivering a good spike as long as I get it! I will try my best to both defend and attack well as long as I am on the court."

After Gong entered the court, Ding Xia passed the first ball to her, who scored a point by making a decisive spike. Then she scored one more point with blocking. As she really played a role soon after entering the match, Gong couldn't help shouting loudly to unleash her emotion before running around the court to make celebration.

The Chinese team began to catch up until the scores were tied at 27-27. At this critical moment, the Netherlands were losing confidence, which led to a serving fault, and a faulty serve receiving resulting in a direct spike. As a result, the Chinese team won the crucial third set with 29-27.

In the fourth set, Gong Xiangyu entered the match as one of the starting players. Although the Netherlands took the lead when the second technical timeout was called, Hui Ruoqi and Gong Xiangyu helped the Chinese team turn the table. When the scores were tied at 23-23, Gong Xiangyu got the match point with a heavy spike.

Next, Hui Ruoqi scored one more point by spiking off the blocking. This helped the Chinese team reach the final with a 3-1 victory over the Netherlands. Zhu scored 33 points in this match, her highest score in a single match of the Olympic Games.

In each of the four sets, the competition was so fierce that the score gap was never really widened. In Lang Ping's words, the score rose alternately, a real test for the Chinese team.

When the moment of victory came, Gong rushed to the courtside and hugged Lang Ping, "Oh my God. I was really scared!" Lang Ping hugged Gong and comforted her, "You performed very bravely. Please do remember this feeling!"

Twelve years had passed before the Chinese team reached the Olympic Final last time. Lang Ping was also continuing her personal legend story. She succeeded in entering the finals in her four-time participation in the Olympic Games as athlete or coach.

11.

It turned out to be the best result.

Five days ago, the Chinese women's volleyball team only ranked the fourth place in the group after losing three matches during the group stage. Without enough confidence in outplaying Brazil, China had prepared to be eliminated in the quarterfinal. To everyone's surprise, it turned out that China defeated Brazil, the host country team, in the quarterfinal. All of a sudden, the prospect of the Chines team in the 2016 Rio Olympic Games became promising.

What's more, in the semifinal Serbia upset the U.S., the team that China felt the least likely to defeat. As China went into the final after ousting the Netherlands, they were to meet Serbia, their final opponent in Rio.

It was the 1198th day since Lang Ping led the Chinese team to embark on the journey towards the Rio Olympic Games.

Coach Lai took out a flag of the Chinese team and a first-day cover featuring the Rio Olympic Games. Then she asked Hui Ruoqi to pass them to the players for their signatures. She and Lang Ping wanted to give them as gifts to an old Polish fan. Since the 2014 Montreux Volley Masters, this man always watched the matches of the Chinese team. This time in Rio, he was present at all the matches with the participation of the Chinese team and cheered for the Chinese team. So, both Coach Lai and Coach Lang wanted to express their gratitude on behalf of the whole team in this way.

To better prepare for the competition with the last opponent Serbia, Lang Ping focused on training the Chinese players' blocking skills. Compared with the previous preparation made for Serbia a week ago, the Chinese girls were obviously more relaxed and had recovered their feeling of how to perform well. The male coaches imitated Serbia's three major spikers, namely, the outside hitter Mihajlovic, the setter Boskovic and the middle blocker Milena Rasic. Though the force of the imitated actions remained unchanged, the Chinese players performed much better in receiving balls.

"On the last day of the competition, only the champion and the third-place winner will be the winners. We must win!"

Even if the Chinese players did their best in the first set, they were still unable to hold off the powerful attacks by Serbia. The Chinese team lost the first set with 19-25.

Lang Ping decisively changed the lineup in the second set. The Chinese players had been enjoying leading advantage of more than five points and made a comeback with 25-17.

The two parties returned to the same starting line. The Serbian team were aggressive and robust while the Chinese team were patient and endurable. Thanks to the points scored by consecutive blockings of Xu Yunli and Hui Ruoqi, the Chinese team gradually widened the lead and carried the match to their advantage. Under the increasing pressure exerted by the blockings of the Chinese players, the two major attackers of the Serbian team made mistakes one after another. The Chinese team were once eight points ahead but the score gap was narrowed to one point later. At 23-22, Zhu Ting, despite the pressure, helped China win the third set by scoring another two points, with a spike and an ace.

In the final stage of the fourth set, the Chinese team reached the "championship point."

The Serbian team requested timeout, and Lang Ping

requested substitution. Zhang Changning, who had been waiting off the court for three sets, was sent to serve the ball. Zhang served brilliantly in the quarterfinal against Brazil and she served the final ball in the semifinal against the Netherlands. However, Lang needed to be bold enough to send Zhang as a substitute for serving.

While Zhang Changning was preparing for serving, other Chinese players were discussing how to perform a good counterattack, how to prepare, what deserved special attention and what tactics to be employed once the ball was served, etc. The six Chinese players in the match completely stayed focused on this ball.

Zhang Changning served a good ball, which was directly dug over the net by the opponent. Hui Ruoqi, well prepared, jumped and made a direct kill.

Seeing that the ball was grounded on the playing court, the players sitting on the bench ran towards their teammates. Only at this moment did Hui Ruoqi come to realize that China really won the championship!

Going through challenges all the way, the unyielding Chinese team won the gold medal at the 2016 Rio Olympic Games after losing the first set but bringing about a complete turnabout in the following three sets.

Everything turned out to be the best arrangement! Even the best scriptwriter could hardly write such an amazing plot full of twists and turns in which there was such an abrupt turnaround in spite of adversity.

No one had expected that during the group stage the Chinese team underperformed. No one had expected that this team could turn the table and rose to the top in Rio in the knockout stage. This should be attributed to their sheer persistence that ultimately gave full play to their great potential in the nip and tuck competitions.

Zhu Ting was the leading scorer in all eight matches of the Chinese team in Rio, scoring a total of 179 points. Her success rate of attacks reached 42.27 percent, a remarkable achievement far ahead of other teams' outside hitters. She was awarded the titles of the Olympic MVP and the Best Outside Spiker.

The volleyball world ushered in the era of the Chinese player Zhu Ting.

Xu Yunli, the oldest and most senior middle blocker, ranked the second in terms of scoring. Lin Li, who joined the national team less than two years ago, was awarded the title of the "Best Libero." All the 12 players got the chance to compete in the court, and they all performed well in the last three showdowns, making their respective contribution to the team's victory.

The Chinese women's volleyball team displayed their long-expected gold medals on the podium at the 2016 Rio Olympic Games. (Photo by Li Zhiyan)

It took Lang Ping and her coach team 40 months to identify and select these players and develop them into a world-class team. All the members of this team made contribution to the new achievements in Rio.

To many people's surprise, Lang Ping didn't shed tears at this peak moment. Instead, she just breathed a sigh of relief as she ultimately fulfilled her mission thanks to the joint efforts of the whole coach team over the previous three and a half years. When the victory came, Lang Ping, an affectionate person, felt grateful to those who had been making contribution to the development of the Chinese team. She said that the Chinese team's victory should be attributed to the joint efforts by so many people.

As Zhu Ting won the Olympic champion title for the first time, she felt that it was like a dream. After putting on the podium-wear, Zhu stood in the aisle, waiting to be awarded the medal. When thinking about how many more Olympic Games she could take part in in the following years, she heard that Wei Qiuyue said to Gong Xiangyu and her: "China will count on you in the next Olympic Games!"

It was not until the gold medal was hung around her neck that Yuan Xinyue believed she was an Olympic champion. "A gold medal weighs about 1.102 pound," Yuan Xinyue and Zhu Ting excitedly exclaimed on the podium: "Heavy! Is it made of genuine gold?" Zhu Ting replied: "Give it a bite and you'll know!"

Watching Zhu and Yuan happily chatting at the award ceremony, Lang Ping exclaimed in delight: "How time flies. These girls have grown up."

CHAPTER FIVE

2017

To start anew

After a triumphant return from the 2016 Rio Olympic Games, Lang Ping began the countdown to her retirement.

On September 30, 2016, in the last hour before Lang Ping retired from the head coach of the Chinese team of the Rio Olympic Cycle, she and her husband Wang Yucheng watched a National Day new film named *Operation Mekong* at a cinema near their home. Before the film began, she sent a text message to her friends: "I won't be the head coach of the Chinese team in an hour. This Olympic cycle really touched me. Thanks for your support! I love you!"

After reading her message, her friends suddenly realized that the "entrepreneurial" journey of the Chinese team led by Lang Ping, the "Iron Hammer", would temporarily come to an end.

All of them had special feelings towards the previous four years, especially the sentiment about bidding farewell to the period full of passion.

At noon on the National Day, Lang Ping had a reunion dinner with her family members and friends. "Now my daughter gets the time to stay with me. I am so happy," said her 83-year-old mother.

Zhu Ting, one of her most outstanding disciples, sent her holiday greetings from Turkey: "Happy National Day, Coach Lang. Thank you for your hard work these years! You've made our Team stronger. In retrospect, so remarkable progress we have made under your guidance."

At that time, Zhu Ting had just joined VakifBank Istanbul, a leading star-studded volleyball club of Turkish Premier League.

As the most expensive Chinese volleyball player of all time, Zhu was eager to prove herself at professional league of the highest level. The head coach of VakifBank Istanbul where Zhu Ting served was Giovanni Guidetti, an Italian veteran who spotted her when she first participated in the Montreux Volley Masters in 2013, her senior international debut.

During the Olympic Games in Rio de Janeiro, there were two fierce competitions between China and the Netherlands. As the head coach of the Netherlands, Guidetti had tried every possible means to restrict Zhu Ting's performance. He could hardly hide his disappointment at the semi-final defeat by the Chinese team. However, to the delight of the young coach, Zhu Ting would join him at the Turkish club after the Olympic Games.

After Rio Olympic Games, the Chinese team began their new journey.

1.

The annual Award Ceremony of Sports Personality of the Year sponsored by CCTV was widely acknowledged as the review, commendation and summary of the Chinese sports circles over the previous year.

Thanks to their continuous progress during the Rio Olympic cycle, the Chinese team led by Lang Ping was the true winner at the award ceremony for the third year in a row.

On January 15, 2017, at the China's Central Television (CCTV) Sports Awards Gala 2016, the Best Coach Award went to Lang Ping. The following day, Lang flew to Chicago, the U.S. to have her right hip joint replaced. (Photo by Li Zhiyan)

After her hip replacement surgery in Chicago, Lang Ping had to begin her tightly-scheduled rehabilitation as soon as possible. She also put some time aside to keep herself updated with the Chinese women's volleyball team online.
(Photo by Liu Xuhui)

Over the next two months, she would take the operation to help alleviate the chronic pain in her right hip joint. At the ceremony, she shook her fist to bolster her courage for her upcoming 11th sports trauma surgery.

At 10 a.m. on January 16, Lang Ping, accompanied by her husband Wang Yucheng, flew to Chicago, the U.S.

Many fans gave their sincere wishes to Lang Ping and wondered if Lang Ping, already a celebrity, would like to lead the Chinese team to compete in the Tokyo Olympic cycle after she recovered from the surgery operation.

Many tried to persuade Lang Ping to go on serving as

the head coach of the Chinese team. She thought for a long time. This was really a difficult decision that was never easier than the one she had made in 2013.

"Four years is really a long cycle, during which the head coach needs to devote himself or herself to the team. I am a very serious-minded person. I always believe that once a decision is made, there can be no retreat. For the sake of my career, I must not make a hasty decision."

In the end, Lang Ping left some leeway in her words: "Personally, I would like to do more for the Chinese team. However, whatever the choice I will make for the next four years, I must first have my hip joints replaced and try to achieve best possible recovery." Her above words were quite reassuring for the Chinese team that would face the challenges from the cycle of the Tokyo Olympic Games.

2.

On April 6, 2017, the Chinese team began their preparation for the Tokyo Olympic Cycle.

Thanks to the two-month recovery after the operation, Lang returned "energetically" as scheduled. However, a month and a half later she was due to have surgery for replacement of her left hip joint. So, she handed her work over to An Jiajie, her assistant coach for the previous three years.

Inside the training hall was the conspicuous new slogan on the opposite wall, which said: "After winning the championship, start from scratch again."

At the beginning of the first training session, Lang Ping, as the head coach of the Chinese team for the Tokyo

Olympic Cycle, gave a speech first. She pointed back to the new slogan on the wall, saying: "We athletes have a saying, 'Start from scratch again from the very moment after getting off the podium.' Eight months have passed after we won Rio Olympic champion. Now we must start anew and begin preparing for the challenges to come during the Tokyo Olympic cycle."

She added: "It's easy to do well for one day or even one week. But it's quite hard to do so for one year. It is even harder to do so for two years, three years or four years. Our greatest wish is to strive for the goal with such fighting spirit on a daily basis."

Inside the training hall was the conspicuous new slogan on the opposite wall, which said: "After winning the championship, start from scratch again." It was quoted from the remarks made by Lang Ping during an awarding ceremony. (Photo by Shi Hui)

It seemed that the above speech marked the kick-off of the Tokyo Olympic cycle.

Zhu Ting was back after winning the Champions and MVPs of CEV Volleyball Champions League - Women and FIVB Volleyball Women's Club World Championship.

After playing for eight months in Europe, Zhu had become stronger, more confident and humorous, and behaved like an international superstar.

As one of the top four foreign players of VakifBank Istanbul, a leading volleyball club of Turkish Premier League, Zhu Ting secured the central role in the team in the first season of her professional career by becoming the best scorer and winning MVP for two times. She fully showed her ability and value as the new captain of the Chinese team.

For Zhu Ting, who was just 22, she needed to both take responsibility and address challenges as captain of the Chinese team.

At the FIVB World Grand Prix, all the leading teams wanted to "challenge" the Chinese team, the Olympic champion, and their captain Zhu Ting, who was said to have become even more powerful after playing for the European Women's Volleyball League.

Zhu appeared much more mature in terms of devotion and determination. She, in a smooth and calm tone, conveyed the confidence of the Chinese team in addressing new challenges in the Tokyo Olympic cycle: "The victory has become the past. Now we must start from scratch again."

3.

The 2017 Women's Grand Champions Cup was the world's highest-ranking volleyball competition in 2017.

Lang Ping, who just had her hip joints of both sides replaced, accompanied the Chinese team for their first competition during the Tokyo Olympic cycle. As soon as Lang entered the gym for their first training session in Japan, she met Nakada Kumi, the head coach of the Japanese women's volleyball team.

They were long-term opponents representing China and Japan respectively in the women's volleyball competition more than 30 years ago.

As soon as Lang Ping and Nakada Kumi met, they had a big hug. Since Nakada Kumi had two years of working experience in Italy, she could speak Italian quite fluently. They began to communicate in Italian.

"You're looking too thin. Have you been too tired lately?" Lang Ping said with concern.

Nakada Kumi helplessly nodded her head: "Yes, there is so much pressure that I can't sleep and eat well."

Lang Ping, also a long-time female head coach on the front line, quite understood the pressure on Nakada Kumi: "You shouldn't go on like this. You need to relax and rest. When the match is over, you must go on holiday and refresh your mind."

They chatted happily for a while. When parting Lang Ping said, "It is great that you are the head coach of the

Japanese team. Now there are two female coaches in the international women's volleyball circle. I won't be standing alone as before."

China and Japan were scheduled to meet in the last match of the 2017 World Grand Champions Cup. However, the Chinese team had secured the champion title in advance before this match.

China outplayed the U.S. and Brazil in the first and second matches 3-1 and 3-2 respectively. Then in Nagoya, they defeated South Korea and Russia, both 3-0. According to the original plan, China would still need to win two sets in their final competition with Japan. Unexpectedly, at the night of September 9, in the fierce competition with the powerful U.S. team, the tenacious Japanese team fought to the tiebreaker. As a result, the Chinese team won the champion title of the 2017 World Grand Champions Cup.

It happened to be the 47th birthday of Lai Yawen, the manager of the Chinese team.

When Lang Ping served as the head coach of that generation of Chinese players including Lai Yawen, she had kept in mind the date of September 9, the birthday of Lai. On the first day upon arrival of the team in Japan, Lang went out to buy Lai a red leather pencil case as her birthday present. Knowing that Lai usually had a lot of deskwork to do, Lang Ping wanted to brighten Lai's life a bit by giving her something interesting and helpful in her routine with heavy workload.

She also bought a beautiful birthday card, asking the Chinese players to write down on the card their respective wishes before sending it to Lai on her birthday.

"Usually, it was Yawen who took care of all the coaches and players and prepared for their birthday celebration.

Today we won the match. Let's celebrate Yawen's birthday together," said Lang Ping.

Back to the hotel from the stadium, Coach Lai felt Lang Ping was planning something with the team members. At the dinner time in the restaurant, when a waiter presented a birthday cake and the whole team sang "Happy Birthday" together, the mystery was discovered. The girls won the 2017 World Grand Champions Cup one round in advance, which was the best birthday present for Coach Lai.

CHAPTER SIX

2018

Though our national anthem couldn't be played, we still could try to have our national flag raised

There was no snow in Beijing this winter.

It was just past the first month of the lunar year. In the previous day it was so warm that one could wear only unlined garments at noon. However, no one had expected that it was so cloudy in the early morning of the following day and soon afterwards snowflakes began to fall.

In the volleyball hall of the Training Bureau of the General Administration of Sports of China, the new-year training camp of the national team had been going on for more than 20 days since the 9th day of the Chinese Lunar New Year.

In the meantime, the Women's Volleyball Super League was in full swing in China. In the two matches before the final, the Shanghai Women's Volleyball Team led by a veteran player and the Tianjin Women's Volleyball Team by a young one both earned landslide victories at each other's home turf. In this best-of-seven series, more wonderful performance was to be expected in the following competitions.

All the players participating in the first-phase training camp came from the teams that failed to make the final four. There were altogether 11 players, in which Ren Kaiyi, Chen Xintong and Zhu Yuezhou were officially included in the national team's training camp list for the first time. Lin Li and Wang Mengjie, who were selected to the Chinese team for the first time in 2015, were indeed veteran players.

On the walls inside the newly decorated training hall were the photos of the Chinese team winning the championship at the 2016 Rio Olympic Games. Accompanied by An Jiajie, Lang Ping recalled the scenes while looking at these photos: "This one of Zhang Changning was about the last rally in Rio, right?"

After a year away, the fitness trainer Rett was back.

Just at a glance, this smart American found that the Chinese slogan on the training hall was different from the one there when he left before the Olympic Games. After understanding what "after winning the championship, start anew again" meant, he really admired the down-to-earth and patient attitude of the Chinese team.

The rehabilitation therapist Daniel had been working in the Chinese team for three years. This taciturn Hawaiian just became a father two months ago. He left his wife and child at home and returned to work in Beijing because he really cared about the Chinese team.

In the second year of the Tokyo Olympic Cycle, all the members of the support team for Chinese team during the Rio Olympic cycle were available. The Chinese team, after one-year adjustment, was about to set off in full force.

2018 was the year for the FIVB Volleyball Women's World Championship.

"This will be a very challenging year in which we need to lay a solid foundation for the Tokyo Olympic Games," said Lang Ping.

1.

From 2013 to 2016, four Chinese players came to fame successively, respectively Zhu Ting in 2013, Yuan Xinyue in 2014, Zhang Changning in 2015, and Gong Xiangyu in 2016.

In the four years of the Rio Olympic cycle, the Chinese team developed a new superstar each year. By 2017, the above four players, all in early twenties, had already become the core members of the Chinese team. People wondered who the next promising new player would be.

Lang Ping and her coaching team were also looking for such players.

Up to 31 players were included in the roster announced by the Chinese team in two stages in 2018. Almost all the players who performed well in the league were called up by the national team. The inclusion of Ren Kaiyi, a university student, and 28-year-old Zhang Yichan, who was selected by the national team for the first time, in particular, showed that the national team were quite open and inclusive in selecting players. This also highlighted Lang Ping's determination to go on building a "big national team" during the Tokyo Olympic cycle.

Of all the newcomers, Li Yingying, an 18-year-old member of the Tianjin Women's Volleyball Team, was the most promising one.

In the exciting and fierce competition for the championship, the two teams respectively from Tianjin and Shanghai fought to the 7th match, which witnessed several times of dramatic changes. The final winner depended on the

Li Yingying (upper), born in 2000, and Zeng Chunlei, born in 1989, were reunited at the national team after facing off against each other for seven sets in the final of the China Women Volleyball League. (Photo by Shi Hui)

performance of the top scorers of the two teams, namely, South Korea's veteran player Kim Yeon-koung and the young player Li Yingying of the generation born in the 2000s.

Before the match started, most people preferred Kim Yeon-koung, a veteran who was more experienced. Unexpectedly, it turned out to be a best-of-seven series and the final score in the deciding set was 16-14. In spite of such stalemate that Li Yingying experienced for the first time, there was nothing of a coward about her. With full support from her teammates, she seized every possible opportunity and decisively handled key points. Finally, The Tianjin Women's Volleyball Team won the championship. The 18-year-old Li Yingying set a single-season scoring new record with 804 points, becoming the youngest MVP in the league.

Soon after winning the league, Li Yingying went to report for duty at the national team.

Then, it was less than a month before the first match of the Chinese team in 2018.

In 2018, the FIVB restructured the FIVB World Grand Prix, the annual international brand competition, as the FIVB Volleyball Women's Nations League (FIVB VNL). The match duration was extended from the original four weeks to seven weeks. The 16 participating teams had to move around five places to compete with another 15 teams within five weeks. After one-week rest, the top five teams and the host country team competed for the finals and the total prize was US$2.2 million.

The changes in the competition arrangement were designed to get the volleyball matches exposed to more cities and more people. This would result in much more wonderful matches. However, the arrangement of personnel, and the reserves and distribution of physical strength posed a new challenge for all participating teams.

Lang Ping took more into consideration.

For example, how to win some matches while training new players? How to better balance the training for the veteran players and new players? How to help the players further realize that they still lag far behind the world's leading teams while boosting their confidence by winning some matches?

Given the fact that the Chinese team began competition without systematic training, Lang Ping warned these who had high expectation that the Chinese team might lose some matches.

2.

Zhu Ting's second season in the Europe league was really "a perfect one".

At the beginning of the season, Giovanni Guidetti, the ambitious head coach of VakifBank Istanbul, pledged that his team would win Turkish Women Volleyball Super Cup, Turkish Cup, Turkey Volleyball Super League and the European Champions League. Almost everyone thought he was just bragging, and no one expected that after eight months of great efforts, VakifBank Istanbul really met all these targets.

At the beginning of the league season, the team won Turkish Women Volleyball Super Cup and Turkish Cup successively. Afterwards, the year of 2018 witnessed the simultaneous participation by Zhu Ting and her teammates in the

Turkish Super League and the European Champions League.

In the Turkish Super League that brought together a large number of the world's top players, each and every post-season match was rather fierce.

In the final title race of the Turkish Super League, VakifBank Istanbul forced into a fifth match against Eczacibasi Vitra Istanbul, a powerful team from the same city. In spite of their failure in the previous competition with the opponent, VakifBank Istanbul ultimately won the fifth match. Zhu Ting scored all the four points leading to the victory of VakifBank Istanbul, winning the first league title in her career. As the champion team's best scorer, Zhu Ting earned the well-deserved MVP.

Then came the quarter finals of the European Champions League. As the defending champion, VakifBank Istanbul, having won all the previous competitions, met their powerful Italian counterpart Imoco Volley Conegliano in the semi-finals. After winning the first two sets, VakifBank Istanbul was tied by the opponent 2-2 after Zhu Ting was substituted because of her sprained ankle. In the deciding set, Zhu Ting once again played a key role and made unparalleled contribution to VakifBank Istanbul's success in defending their title of the European Champion.

In the European Champions League this year, Zhu played 12 matches for VakifBank Istanbul, ranking the first place among the top scorers with 229 points. Her total spike success rate and efficiency reached 53.87% and 43.84% respectively, well ahead of other players in the world-class European Champions League. Moreover, she also broke the record set by herself in the previous year.

During the first year of Zhu's working abroad, Lang Ping encouraged her: "Compete in the overseas playing court and try to win worldwide acclaim." Zhu Ting really did it.

On May 10, Zhu Ting, after working abroad for two years, arrived in Beilun together with the team manager Lai Yawen.

"I was very excited on the way to Beilun, imagining what Coach Lang and other team members were doing at the very moment when I walked into the training hall." Zhu Ting said merrily: "I haven't seen them for seven months. I really miss them all."

However, Lang decided to give Zhu a vacation after having the team's group photo taken.

"After so long a time of highly intensive competitions, Zhu needs to have a good rest and relax herself."

3.

In 2018, unexpectedly, all of a sudden there came the failure.

In the third round of the FIVB VNL, the Chinese women's volleyball team met again the South Korean women's volleyball team led by Kim Yeon-koung. Since the 2015 Asian Women's Volleyball Championship final and the FIVB Volleyball Women's World Cup, the two teams had two fierce competitions. The Chinese team won both matches, which allowed them to enjoy psychological advantage over South Korea. What's more, China upset South Korea 3-0 in the 2017 World Grand Champions Cup. As a result, no one doubted that the Chinese team would win over South Korea easily.

Lang Ping, however, didn't think so. "The starting lineup

of the South Korea is almost the same as that at the 2015 Asian Women's Volleyball Championship. If their potential is given to full play, I am afraid it will pose great challenges for our young players."

In the morning of the match, the Chinese team were unusually late for field practice by 10 minutes, for Lang Ping "stayed late" during the video study session before the departure. Worrying that the younger players didn't get well prepared for the powerful attacks by the South Korean veterans, she wanted to give the Chinese players more instructions.

After the training, the Chinese team returned to the hotel restaurant for dinner. When Lang Ping was thinking about more options of arrangement for the match in the evening, she found Li Yingying passing by with a plate of fried chicken and chips.

"Yingying, is this your lunch?" Lang Ping was a little shocked.

"Yes, my favorite!" Li Yingying felt very happy as she hadn't eaten such foods for a long time.

Believing that Yingying must be hungry after a training course, Lang Ping, instead of speaking great truths, said "Now, you go to get another plate. Just follow me in choosing foods."

After lunch, Lang Ping went to Rett, the fitness trainer, asking him to measure Li's body fat and come up with a plan to reduce her body fat and urge her to begin practice as soon as possible.

As expected by Lang Ping, in the competition between China and South Korea in the evening, Kim Yeon-koung fully leveraged her understanding of Li Yingying based on their competitions in the China Women Volleyball League. The

South Korean players focused on defending the attacks by Li Yingying from the very beginning and two of her three spikes were blocked.

Volleyball competition was really a tough test for players. New players, in particular, often underperformed due to certain weakness.

Just in her third match on behalf of the national team, Li Yingying was under such a test: her attacks were blocked; the ball she served went out of the court; she failed to receive the serve; and she couldn't block the ball properly.

At the mid of the second set, Li Yingying was substituted. After resting for a while, she felt refreshed. Unexpectedly, only after scoring a point by spiking in the third set, something was wrong with her blocking. Li Yingying, the best volleyball player of the generation born in the 2000s, demonstrated overwhelming power and skill in the China Women Volleyball League. She never expected she underperformed at the international playing court. This really made her frustrated.

Lang, however, remained patient. She told reporters at a press conference: "Li Yingying just began her career in the national team. Please don't put too much pressure on her. We need to remain patient as she still has a long way to go."

Confidence is something quite strange, which can hardly be grasped.

Given the fact that the Chinese team were scheduled to compete against Poland, Thailand and Serbia in Macau in the second week, Lang Ping was immediately asked by reporters if Zhu Ting would be called back in advance. Lang Ping answered this question with her facial expressions, indicating "why to do so?"

"Zhu Ting is on vacation, and Zhang Changning has fallen ill. This happens to be good chance for these new players and other veteran team members to improve their skills. The following matches will be even difficult. The Chinese team will inevitably lose some of them. We need to learn from the matches and identify our weakness. We just need to keep improving ourselves. In fact, we are not as powerful as you thought, and we need to keep improving through training and competition."

It seemed that Lang Ping had been fully prepared for the upcoming challenges.

In the match with Poland in Macau, Lang insisted on keeping Li Yingying on the court. In this match, Li Yingying played well in terms of attack, scoring 19 points, the highest one in the team. However, she was relatively deficient in blocking, defence and serve receiving.

When asked about Li Yingying's scoring 19 points at the post-match press conference, Lang Ping made the following remark frankly:

"I don't care too much about any specific aspect of one player's technical skills. An excellent outside hitter must be an all-round player. It is the first time that Li Yingying participated in this kind of competition. This allows her to identify quite some vulnerabilities in her technical skills. She should resolve to make improvements. We shouldn't overestimate our domestic China Women Volleyball League. In fact, many Chinese players will find the huge gap between them and their overseas counterparts when they compete in the world-class competitions."

She said that Chinese players should make more efforts to catch up.

4.

After the Tokyo Olympic Cycle began, the Italian team rekindled the hope of dominating the women volleyball circle thanks to the emergence of Paola Ogechi Egonu, a tall girl with amazing leaping ability.

As expected, the Italian women's volleyball team were reshuffled for the 2017 Tokyo Olympic Preparation Cycle. After making sustainable progress in the league, Egonu became the core spiker with even more aggressive and powerful skills.

In the third week of the FIVB VNL, China and Italy met in the competition held in Hong Kong, China. At this point, Captain Zhu Ting had returned to the national team. In the first two match days, China outplayed Argentina and Japan twice 3-0. Since the Italian team were in the same group as the Chinese team in group stage of the FIVB Volleyball Women's World Championship, the Chinese players wanted to take this chance to learn more about the opponent's actual strength and hoped to enhance their confidence by winning this match. However, from the very beginning of the match, the Chinese team were forced into a passive position: The opponents focused on weakening the strength of Zhu Ting, whose attacks were blocked or defended one after another. On the other side of the net, the high hit by Egonu was so powerful that Italy won two sets in a row 25-18 and 25-14.

The Chinese team changed their offensive tactics in the third set, which helped them win this set with 25-16. However, the Italian team, after quickly adapting to China's tactical changes, launched fierce attacks again in the fourth set. Suppressed by the attacks of Paola Ogechi Egonu and

Miryam Fatime Sylla, the Chinese team lost this set with 18-25. As a result, they lost this match 1-3.

Upon hearing Lang Ping's words after the match, the Chinese team members realized that just after two years, the Chinese team were losing the advantage over Italy. Unexpectedly, this really posed a great challenge to China.

"We can hardly effectively defend the attacks by Egonu, player No. 18 of the opponent. She is really unique in her skills and is featured by very high hit. This will also be the focus of our training from now on."

On the way forward, challenges always came one after another. There was rather limited time left for Lang Ping and her team.

5.

Of all the 12 matches within one month, the Chinese team only won six of them, losing all the matches with their major opponents including the United States, Brazil, Italy and Serbia.

Only when half of the matches were completed in the Jiangmen leg, Lang Ping decided to let An Jiajie lead the young Chinese players for the matches in Stuttgart in the 5th week, while she herself would take the key players to Beijing for training.

There was just two weeks left before the final of the FIVB VNL to be held in Nanjing. In addition, the Asian Games and the FIVB Volleyball Women's World Championship, another two major events, were on their ways.

Lang Ping was under so great pressure as soon as the national team season began. She was so exhausted that she peaked and pined within four weeks. Her friends really worried about her health.

However, Lang Ping was as optimistic and humorous as ever: "I am fine. Every day I go to bed at 2 or 3 o'clock a.m. and get up at 7 o'clock in the morning. This year our task will focus on training young players. I have to say that so far I am the one that has improved the most!"

Back in Beijing, Lang Ping couldn't wait to take her luggage home before having her hair cut. As soon as the hair was cut, all her white hair hidden beneath was exposed. The hairdresser advised her to dye her hair again, but she refused because she had to go back to the Athlete Apartments. "My players are waiting for me there!"

It was the repeated practice of basic skills and the perfect teamwork that resulted in the impressive performance of the Chinese team over the previous years. It was until the mid-April that almost all players were gathered together. Even worse, some players needed to have their injuries treated and their strength restored first. The Chinese team would be at a disadvantage if it competed with opponents in terms of physical fitness and skills without practicing training and teamwork drills.

"Then let's hurry up and practice even hard!" Lang Ping didn't want to delay training.

As the training began, the girls kept their eyes on the ball, the speed of which was so fast that they felt the ball was about to be grounded on the court as soon as it shot out of the serving machine. Lin Li had adapted herself to such challenges as she had to receive over a hundred of such balls every day during the training period. Therefore, the first set of balls served by the serving machine mainly targeted at the direction of Lin Li.

When it was Zhu Ting's turn, she would rub her slender forearms after receiving each ball. For any ordinary person, digging a ball with his or her forearm will cause the ache. The forearms will turn red after several times of forearm digging. After one day of continuous practice, she would find that her arms might swell up the next day. These Chinese players had to dig with their forearms the balls that shot towards them at an hourly speed of 100 kilometers. What's more, they were required to dig the ball to the designated area, otherwise it was disqualified.

After a set of training, Liu Xiaotong could not help but open the black protective sleeves to check her arms. As she was absent from systematic training this year, she had not received balls served from serving machine for a long time. At this moment she felt a kind of burning sensation in her forearms inside the nylon protective sleeves. Her teammates took a close look and found there were many imprints of redness in her forearms, some of which had signs of extravasated blood.

"Remember to treat your forearms with ice compress immediately after the training. Then apply hot compress in the evening. Otherwise, how can you expect to go on training tomorrow?" Lin Li was the most experienced in this aspect.

At the end of the training, when Liu Xiaotong and Zhu Ting iced their forearms, Doctor Wei was helping Yan Ni tear off several layers of adhesive plasters tightly wrapped around her right arm.

After a training class, the adhesive plasters became stuck more tightly to the skin due to sweat infiltration. Tearing off each piece of plaster would cause intolerable pain for Yan Ni.

"It is the same case every day and I'm used to it. I have to wrap plasters in the morning and tear them off in the evening. This has caused my skin to become allergic and very rough."

Even so, she didn't give up.

During the finals in the last week of June, the Chinese team significantly improved their performance. China finally won the second runner-up in the FIVB VNL. This should be attributed to their tactics of focusing on training new players regardless of the possibilities of losing the matches, and their practice of identifying problems and paying special attention to details. However, this really made the Chinese players fatigued.

6.

On July 2, Lukou Airport, Nanjing, Zhang Changning, after over two months of recovery from a medical operation, joined the national team here and flew back to Beijing.

With her return, the starting lineup of the Chinese women's volleyball team became complete. In mid-August, the Chinese team participated in Jakarta Asian Games, for which their main opponents including Japan, South Korea and Thailand all sent their main lineups. Their strength should never be underestimated. After returning from Indonesia to China in early September, the Chinese team sent a squad to the Montreux Volley Masters. Then on September 25, they would take part in the FIVB Volleyball Women's World Championship.

Unluckily, the Chinese team, the runner-up of the previous year's FIVB Volleyball Women's World Championship and the team of the world's first-place ranking, this time was placed in the "group of top teams" and "the pool of many top teams". This was because Italy and Turkey were in the same group as the Chinese team. These two teams, though not enjoying high world rankings, had been making rapid progress over the previous year. Even worse, in the pool where the Chinese team were in, there also included Russia that had great potential and the United States that the Chinese team never won over the several previous years. If the Chinese team failed to rank the top three in these five teams, they would be eliminated from the top six. This meant that they had no chance of standing on the podium and, let alone achieve a "Three-peat".

Despite the fact that the Chinese team didn't perform well in 2018, the public still had high expectation for their performance at the following FIVB Volleyball Women's World Championship. If the Chinese team led by Lang Ping could win the FIVB Volleyball Women's World Championship in 2018, they would achieve a "Three-peat" including the FIVB Volleyball Women's World Cup, Olympic Games and the FIVB Volleyball Women's World Championship. If this came true, Lang Ping would become the first person that won "Three-peat" both as player and coach.

This was really a grand goal. However, what Lang Ping and her coaching team were concerned about was how to better prepare for the two important matches by making good use of the limited time. They needed to accomplish the task as best as possible, and properly distribute the athletes' physical strength, adjust their performance and avoid unnecessary injuries.

On July 15, the Chinese team went to Beilun again to begin the one-month training camp in 2018.

In order to put aside more time for training, Lang Ping

brought the team members into the gym at 7:30 every morning to start the morning training for strengthening their basic skills. In the 45-minute morning training, the groups of receivers, setters and middle blockers were arranged respectively. The whole team gathered at 8:15 a.m. The morning training lasted until 1:00 p.m. After lunch, the players snatched a rest after taking a bath. The afternoon training started at 3:30 p.m. and went on until 7:00 p.m. They held a meeting at 8 p.m. and studied the main opponents to be met in the Asian Games and the FIVB Volleyball Women's World Championship. Then they began receiving physical therapy treatment after 9:30 p.m.

The training camp was so intensive and demanding that at the end of the day the players just wanted to fall into bed at once.

"The alarm clock woke me up at 6:15 a.m. I was so sleepy that I brushed my teeth with my eyes closed." Rubbing her eyes that were screwed up, Liu Xiaotong went to the dining room for breakfast and saw Lang Ping smiling at her. "I was immediately awakened by Coach Lang who was enormously energetic. She woke up earlier than us but went to bed later than us. She led the training throughout the whole process and even seldom sat down. Though at young age, we were so exhausted at the end of the training, not to mention Coach Lang. We really worried about her health."

All Chinese players knew that when Lang Ping coached the Chinese team for the first time, she once fainted in the training hall and was taken to the hospital by ambulance due to overwork. Seeing Lang Ping working so hard in coaching them, the players really worried about her health. However, they realized that devotion to the training would be the best approach to helping alleviate her pressure.

During the one-month training camp in Beilun, the

Chinese team focused on improving their basic skills and fitting in the squad. As the Chinese team were well prepared, they won the championship of the Asian Games without losing one set throughout all the eight matches. Although it was just the Asian champion, it helped boost the morale of the Chinese team that had been at a low ebb over the previous months of the year.

7.

This was the fifth Asian Games in which Lang Ping took part. It was a time span of forty years, from 1978 when she represented the Chinese women's volleyball team for the first time, to her celebrating her 18th birthday at the Bangkok Asian Games, to 1998 when 38-year-old Lang Ping led the Chinese team to compete in Bangkok, and to 2018 when 58-year-old Lang Ping led the Chinese team for the Asian Games in Jakarta.

Seeing Lang Ping sitting on the coach bench of the Chinese team at this Asian Games, many fans felt that she was becoming old. However, when Lang Ping wore the same uniform as that of the Chinese players and had a broad smile spreading across her face, they also felt she was still as attractive as before—because she had been sticking to her cause out of love.

After her team winning the championship of the Asian Games, Lang Ping revealed what she really thought for the first time since 2018.

> "This is your fifth time of your participation in the Asian Games. Will you take part in the sixth one?"
>
> Lang Ping: "I can participate in it as a member of

the visiting group."

"As for the five Asian Games you participated in, you won a silver medal and a gold medal as an athlete and three gold medals as a coach. Do you have a lot of memories about the Asian Games?"

Lang Ping (smilingly): "The time span is so long that my memory is fading. I am most impressed by the event of this year."

"In this Asian Games, the Chinese team won all the eight matches with 3-0. It seemed that you made it very easily. However, the fans who followed the Chinese team knew your team and you had gone through a lot of hardship and challenges in the preparation process."

Lang Ping: "We played eight matches in the Asian Games. In fact, there were only three matches in which our opponents could rival us. We played well and won all of them 3-0. However, if we were not so well prepared or didn't perform that well, it would be very tough for us to make it. We will inevitably regret for the match we lost that we shouldn't have lost due to our mistakes and mentality fluctuation. Therefore, I always say that we must try our best to fulfill our obligations. We should never be afraid of hard work or trouble."

"The FIVB Volleyball Women's World Championship will begin in less than one month. What do you think of the challenges?"

Lang Ping: "There are many opponents in the World Championship. The Chinese team will face severe challenges in the group stage. Our task is to make sound preparation and try our best to improve ourselves for the purpose of performing well in every match."

"We are all looking forward to your leading the Chinese team to a new 'Three-peat'."

Lang Ping: "Among the top teams in the world, the Chinese team ranks the sixth or seventh place in terms of real strength. We need to make continuous progress in training and try to narrow the gap with the world's leading teams. Placed in the group of many powerful opponents, we have to figure out how to survive the group stage and secure a place among the top six. As for the 'Three-peat', expected by many, this shouldn't distract us from our focus on our training."

8.

On September, 25, 2018, the Chinese women's volleyball team began competing at the FIVB Volleyball Women's World Championship.

Compared with the previous competitions, the preparation made by the Chinese team this time seemed to be somewhat in a hurry. During the limited three-week training camp, the Chinese players mainly focused on studying the two main opponents in the group stage. They worked together to thoroughly analyze the situation, concluding that they must win the match against Turkey in the second match day, otherwise they would have a very fierce competition with Italy. If they lost, they might be eliminated from the top six after the group stage.

Just like what they did during the "Brazilian month" and "American month" before the Olympic Games, the Chinese coaches thoroughly analyzed videos of the opponent and studied them item by item. After digesting and absorbing all the relevant information, the coaches began to instruct the team members on studying and practicing relevant expertise. During the training process, they will further study and figure out new solutions once any new problem was identified. However, three weeks was so limited that they could hardly make a thorough analysis of their two main opponents.

On the eve of the match, while packing up, Lang Ping double-checked with An Jiajie if they had carried all their research documents concerning opponents with them. She joked, "You can buy anything but these documents, because they are invaluable assets. If you forget to take them, you may have to fly back to get them."

Zhang Changning, who was injured one and a half months ago, finally secured herself a place in the FIVB Volleyball Women's World Championship. However, given her less ideal performance and limited physical reserve, no one had high expectation for her.

"There will be tough matches ahead of us," Coach Lang said to Coach Lai at Beijing Capital International Airport as she looked at the 14 players who would compete for the FIVB Volleyball Women's World Championship. "Let's try our best day by day."

Giovanni Guidetti led the Netherlands women's volleyball team to win the best ever achievement in the Rio Olympic Games. What's more, only one year after becoming the head coach of the Turkish team, he developed this team into a powerful one with the strongest attacking ability.

It was Zhu Ting who helped Giovanni Guidetti to establish a closer relationship with China. After the 2016 Rio Olympic Games, Zhu went to Turkey to play for VakifBank Istanbul, a leading team coached by Giovanni Guidetti.

During the two years, he took good care of Zhu Ting, which won him popularity among Chinese fans.

On the second match day of the FIVB Volleyball Women's World Championship, the Chinese team met Turkish team. As both sides were eager to win, it was widely predicted before the match that the competition would be rather fierce.

The Chinese team had given high priority to this match when making plans for the World Championship. After all, the match outcome at the beginning stage of the World Championship was of critical importance for securing confidence, morale and advancement to the next stage.

"Before every match starts, the odds are always 50-50." Lang Ping told the players and responded to the media in this way. "So, we must start well and hold them down. If the Turkish team find the chance to give full play to their potential, we will be in trouble."

Zhu Ting was fully aware that Giovanni Guidetti and several Turkish players knew her very well from their two-year cooperation at VakifBank Istanbul. Therefore, she was not only ready to be restrained, but also had figured out how to launch counterattack.

As expected, the first ball served by the Turkish player was targeted at Zhu Ting. They also tried to cheer themselves up from the very beginning. In the meantime, several attacks by Zhu were defended by Turkish players. Fortunately, with a plan in mind, Zhu took the initiative to seek different tactics. This helped the Chinese team further widen the score gap and succeed in keeping the opponent down.

At the Montreux Volley Masters a month ago, Turkish team showed very high proficiency during the matches. However, contrary to their high morale at the beginning of this match, they began losing confidence and making more faults under the increasing pressure from China. The volleyball matches are, besides a competition of strength, an arena for suppression versus counter-suppression.

Through excellent service, combined with blocking, the Chinese team overwhelmed the ambitious Turkish team. They earned a landslide 3-0 victory over the Turkish team, passing the group stage of the World Championship.

Giovanni Guidetti had to accept their failure. However, he felt somewhat relieved at the idea that it was Zhu Ting, his favorite player at VakifBank Istanbul club, who helped China win this match.

When the two teams shook hands after the match, he was courting Zhu Ting, who pretended to show her displeasure and said, "Why almost all the balls served were targeted at me?"

Giovanni Guidetti smiled cunningly. "I didn't mean it!"

"You did it on purpose!" Zhu Ting joked with him as she was in a good mood after winning the match.

Zhu Ting received team-high 18 first pass in the whole match and had 15 kills in 29 attempts plus one blocking to lead China with 16 points.

When sitting at the courtside after the match, the players gave thumbs up to their trainers, who were in charge of their training, praising them for their wonderful imitation of actions of the Turkish outside hitters. This allowed the Chinese players to quickly adapt themselves to the technical skills of the opponents in this match.

"It was a crucial victory that helped greatly boost our morale." Lang Ping concluded, "We fought together, and the victory should be attributed to the joint efforts of our team."

9.

In the final round of group stage, China and Italy competed for the top spot in Group B. Italy enjoyed an advantage over China in terms of players' availability for various positions and their competitive performance. The records of their matches during the two years of Tokyo Olympic cycle also showed that the Italian team won most of the competitions.

Lang Ping required her players to "score every point bit by bit", which indicated the great challenge posed by the match.

The Chinese team didn't perform well at the beginning of the match, lagging behind their opponent with 2-5 due to successive faults. However, instead of being nervous, the Chinese players insisted on encouraging each other, hoping to catch up with the opponent as soon as possible. With Zhang Changning successfully piercing the blocking, the Chinese team soon tied the score. The two sides entered the stalemate stage.

The Chinese team focused on blocking the attacks by Paola Ogechi Egonu, the ace spiker of the Italian team.

The first set saw the two teams tie 8-8 as Yan Ni managed to block the attack by Egonu, scoring a point crucially important for boosting the moral of Chinese players. Seeing the efforts made for studying the opponent before the match proved to be effective during this match, even the substitute players couldn't help jumping to their feet out of joy.

"Monster block! Monster block!" Under a uniform rhythm,

the spectators cheered for Yan Ni's wonderful blocking.

Yan Ni's confidence was furthered inspired. She once again blocked the next round of attack launched by the Italian team.

As a result, Egonu, the capable spiker, became hesitant and made more mistakes. Miryam Fatime Sylla, another top-notch player, could hardly exert her offensive threat as the ball served by the Chinese players continuously targeted at her.

When the Chinese team led by 16-13, Sylla was substituted in the back row.

As a result, Egonu and Sylla, the two main scorers, were both restricted. Such case might be the first time for the Italian team that had gone very well over the previous year.

Due to their adequate preparation, the Chinese team held down the aggressive Italian team with effective blocking, defence and coordination. In sharp contrast to Egonu and Sylla's helplessness, the Chinese players remained sober and calm. The Chinese team won the first set 25-20, which was really an amazing opening.

From the beginning of the second set, the Italian team performed much better in the cooperation between their attack and defence. The Chinese team kept up the same strategy by going on serving mainly with Sylla as the target and trying to block the attacks by Egonu. After withstanding the opponent's powerful attacks during the starting stage and being lagging behind three points at most, the Chinese team had been maintaining a narrow lead over the opponent until the mid of the set.

Unexpectedly, although the two black wing spikers underperformed, the two tall Italian middle blockers gave full play to their great potential.

Although the Chinese team tried to catch up with the opponent in the competitions for key points at the end of the set, the Italian team managed to win this set 26-24.

As soon as the last ball of this set was grounded on the playing court, Cristina Chirichella turned around and roared on her knees, while the other Italian players gathered around to celebrate the hardest victory of this set. Even the Italian coach who ran up on the stage to collect match statistics couldn't help but dance with excitement.

The decisive score at the end of the second set marked a turning point of the match between China and Italy.

In the third and fourth sets, as the Italian team performed even better on both defence and attack, the insufficient attack points of the Chinese team were further highlighted. Zhang Changning, Li Yingying and Liu Xiaotong all tried their best on the court. However, none of them could cooperate well enough with Zhu Ting.

Lang tried various combinations of wing spikers, which included the attempts to place Zhang Changning on the position of opposite in the fourth set. However, the Chinese players at this moment were not as clear-headed and well-organized as they had been in the first set. Lang Ping's various attempts did not work out as expected. Facing the high-level blocking of Italy, all the Chinese players, except Zhu Ting, could hardly pierce the blocking of the opponents.

After the match, the match statistics showed that the points scored by the blocking of the Chinese and Italian teams were 9 and 19 respectively.

The Chinese team lost two sets in a row 16-25 and 20-25. As a result, they had a 1-3 defeat against Italy.

This failure left too much regret because the result might

be different given the following assumptions: For example, if the Chinese team could win the last few crucial points at the end of the second set; if the Chinese team could perform well in serve receiving during the final two sets; if Zhang Changning could better perform in the position of opposite.

While relaxing themselves on the court after the match, the Chinese players gathered in twos and threes, exchanging ideas in a low voice. The coaches pointed out some specific problems. Instead of feeling frustrated, they learned from this match that they had done many things right in the preparation process.

On October 5th, the Chinese team took an early flight from Sapporo to Osaka, where there would be four tough matches ahead for them.

"I always encourage our players to be on the bright side of life, so everyone will become more motivated." Lang Ping always took the lead in fulfilling her requirements for the players. She added that, as a result, she had formed the habit of always being optimistic after all these years.

10.

It was 12 years ago that the Chinese team upset the United States in one of the three major world matches.

China outplayed the U.S. 3-1 during the 2006 FIVB Volleyball Women's World Championship. Since then, China haven't won the United States even when they won the FIVB Volleyball Women's World Cup and the Olympic champion in 2015 and 2016 respectively.

When the Chinese team met the U.S. team again in the

match before the final in the 2018 FIVB Volleyball Women's World Championship, it was widely believed that they were not capable enough to win this match.

"No matter how strong the opponent is, I will try my best to win. If I can win this time, I won't wait until the next time." It wasn't until the Chinese team unexpectedly enjoyed the landslide victory over their American counterpart that Lang Ping revealed her mind.

During the closed training on the rest days and the match day, Lang Ping led the team to make preparation and deployment for the upcoming match with their American counterpart. She always mobilized her players to maintain a good mood, encouraging them to deal with the opponent patiently with the right mindset.

Lang Ping didn't deliberately emphasize results. "I hope everyone will try to find a way to deal with the opponent from her own point of view. All the efforts we are making aimed at upsetting the opponent in the end."

During the warming up before the match, the Chinese players looked relaxed.

From the beginning of the match, they performed quite aggressively. Their thorough and detailed study and preparation were fully demonstrated in their serving performance, landing points, coordination of blocking, and defensive position, etc. Based on the uniform strategy, the players strictly followed the coach's plan.

After the Chinese team won the first set 25-17, the U.S. players began to cheer up and exerted more pressure on their Chinese counterparts, especially after Kelly Murphy was substituted by Karsta Lowe. After fierce competition, China ultimately won this set 26-24.

"Well done! You performed well as a whole, except for the last few points in the second set that somewhat aroused our worry." Lang Ping summed it up this way humorously after a 3-0 win.

In the whole match, the Chinese team had only one substitution. Hu Mingyuan replaced Yan Ni to serve the ball. But the seven starting players and seven substitutes worked so well.

After winning the match, on their way back to the hotel, the physical trainer Rett had a group photo of the Chinese team on the bus to celebrate the important victory.

When the national anthem of the United States was played before the match, Rett, standing in the stands of the Chinese team and putting his right hand on his left chest, sang with the anthem. He was as happy as a lark when China ultimately won the United States.

The Chinese team included experts from the United States who made long-term contributions. Their great efforts were highly appreciated.

Twenty years ago, Lang Ping wrote in her autobiography named *Legends of the Youth*: "We compete in the world match instead of fighting a world war. Instead of fighting for profits, we aim to show the human spirit."

After more than 40 years of development, the Chinese team have become more diversified and enjoyed more interesting stories.

11.

During the matches of the Final Six stage, the Chinese team met their American counterpart in Nagoya again.

Three days ago, the long-term defeat of the Chinese team in their competition with the United States came to an end. However, besides their full preparation and excellent performance, should the Chinese team's 3-0 landslide victory over the United States be attributed to the fact that the U.S. team underestimated China? Did the Chinese team really find a way to effectively compete against the U.S. team?

This will be tested by the following competition between them.

In the last round of the playoff, the Chinese team still tried their best to upset their Russian counterpart even though they had secured a place among the top six. This was the result most expected by the U.S. team.

Two hours later, the draw results for the final six was unveiled. China, the United States and the Netherlands were placed in the same pool. The competition between China and the U.S. began first.

The U.S. team didn't expect that they would compete with China again so soon. In comparison, it was easier for the American players to adjust their state of mind than their counterpart because the previous 3-0 competition had put the Chinese team under the spotlight.

"I think that after a three-day thorough study, the U.S. team must have figured out more specific tactics against us. We won't go as smoothly as we did in the last match. We'd better prepare for a 5-set match." Lang Ping reminded her players at the pre-match preparation meeting.

Lai Yawen added: "We must pay special attention to the key points. The final result may hinge on these key points."

Their highlights of the following match between China and the United States turned out to be what the two veterans had predicted before the match.

The Coach Karch Kiraly adjusted his starting lineup by rearranging the first-pass cooperation where they underperformed in the previous match. The U.S. team got off to a good start. In contrast, the Chinese team didn't play well enough in minimizing their faults, which resulted in their poor performance at the beginning.

At the end of the first set, Zhu Ting played to her strength, helping the Chinese team to tie at 20-20 and further win this set 25-22. This success fully boosted the confidence of the Chinese players. However, no one had expected the counterattack of the U.S. team came so quickly.

In the previous match, the victory of the Chinese team over their American counterpart should be mainly attributed to their tactics of scoring based on multiple positions. Gong Xiangyu who scored 14 points played a critically important role. However, in this match, under the great pressure of powerful middle blockers of the U.S. team, Gong Xiangyu no longer performed so well. As a result, Gong was somewhat less confident, especially after her attacks were blocked in a row. Despite all their great efforts, the Chinese team still lost two sets 19-25 and 20-25.

"As the U.S. team have the upper hand, we have to push our way through it." When lagging behind 1-2, Lang Ping reminded her players, "It doesn't matter. Don't worry. We must stick to it."

In the fourth match, the Chinese team had no alternative but to change the lineup. The veteran player Zeng Chunlei and new player Li Yingying were sent onto the court. This was the first time that two starting players were changed at the same time since the beginning of the FIVB Volleyball Women's World Championship.

Before Zeng Chunlei and Li Yingying went into the court, Lang Ping said to them: "Fight! We have no other choice! We had to forge ahead and look for opportunities!"

In the first half of the set, the Chinese team gained the upper hand, with five points ahead at most. However, at the end of the set, they continuously lost rallies to the opponent, which was exerting increasingly growing pressure on the Chinese players.

At this critical moment, Lang Ping replaced Zeng Chunlei with Yao Di and Ding Xia with Gong Xiangyu.

"Even if we ultimately lost, we must never give in!" Lang Ping said to Lai Yawen who was sitting next to her.

The two points that decided the outcome of the whole match were scored by Li Yingying, who participated in such a world-class match for the first time. The Chinese team tied the set score 2-2.

Everyone was happy to see that the potential of Li Yingying was fully tapped. This meant that one more powerful spiker was added to the Chinese team. As a result, Lang Ping had more options available for her lineup.

After winning the fourth set, Xu Yunli, sitting on the athletes' bench, predicted, "I think we can win!"

"It's the tradition of the Chinese team to help each other and complement each other's weaknesses," said Xu

Yunli, "Although only Zhu Ting was among the best in terms of individual ability, no team can rival the Chinese team in teamwork."

Zhu Ting added that the joint efforts of all 14 players were quite extraordinary.

The Chinese team won their American counterpart twice within three days. Rett took a group photo of the Chinese players on the bus again in celebration of their victory. Compared with that in the photo taken after the previous 3-0 rematch, the smiles in this photo were brighter.

In the second match of the Final Six stages, the Chinese team topped Group F with a 3-1 victory over the Netherlands.

Though the Chinese team outplayed their American counterpart for two times, their American physical trainer Rett (R1), in good mood, had a group photo of the Chinese team on the bus to celebrate the important victory.
(Photo by Rett)

From Nagoya to New Yokohama, they met Italy again in the semi-finals.

12.

The 2018 FIVB Volleyball Women's World Championship was the seventh one for Lang Ping.

It has been 23 days since September 25, when the match began. The Chinese team has played 11 matches in four different places. The long World Championship would come to an end soon.

At 3:00, October 19, the semi-final match between China and Italy kicked off.

More than 60 percent of the fans present were supporters of the Chinese team, who formed squares in red behind the Chinese team's coach bench. Even before the match began, the two stands in the middle had become a sea of red.

Both sides were more fully prepared for this match compared with that during the matches of group stage. However, the Chinese team were at a disadvantage. Zhang Changning just recovered from her injuries and didn't resume her systematic training. She had to keep on playing until the 12th match when her physical reserves were no longer sufficient. Therefore, although she was still capable of handling serve receiving, she could hardly provide strong support for Zhu Ting as required in terms of attacking. Trailing at 12-19, China's head coach Lang Ping sent Li Yingying onto the court in replacement of Zhang Changning. However, the Chinese team still lost the first set with 7 points behind.

In the second set, the Chinese team kept their morale

rising gradually. This helped them keep a narrow lead until the end of the set. At 23-21, Hu Mingyuan, who participated in the world match for the first time on behalf of China, was sent onto the court to serve the ball. It was her two consecutive aces that helped the Chinese team win the second set. Both Hu's composure and Lang's courage were quite impressive.

After losing the third set 16-25, it was very likely that the Chinese team would lose this match.

In the crucial fourth set, the Chinese team maintained a lead of about two points during most of the time. However, when the score came near to 20, the Italian team tried to tie the score and further surpassed the score with strong blocking. When Italy led 23-21 at the end of the fourth set, the Chinese team tied the score with two attacks by Zhu Ting and Gong Xiangyu. China further reached the set point after the ball served by Zhu Ting broke the opponents' serve receiving and the ball spiked by Egonu went out of the court.

The competition was so fierce that the two teams sank into a seesaw match until 29-29. With indomitable will and unyielding spirit, the Chinese team held out until the end of this set. The decisive point that sealed the victory of this set was scored by Zhu Ting, who made the spike after making adjustment. The Official Review showed the ball was grounded on the line.

31-29! The Chinese team won the fourth set.

Such resilient spirit demonstrated by the young generation of Chinese players moved many Chinese fans present to tears. If the Chinese team further won the deciding set, the rather fierce competition in the fourth set would certainly become one of the most dramatic parts on their way to the championship.

However, it was not this case…

In the deciding set, China managed to tie at 14-14 and 15-15 from 12-14. However, at last China lost this crucial set by two points.

As for the last ball, the two sides had multiple rallies. When the attack by Egonu spiked off the blocking, Zhu Ting, standing in the back row, looked in the direction that the ball went out. Her helpless eyes indicated that she felt sorry for the failure of the Chinese team. The score finally stopped at 17-15. The Italian players wept with joy, while the Chinese ones felt dejected.

It was at that moment that they further understood the cruelty of competitive sports.

The Chinese team, once the Olympic champion, stopped on the way to the final of the FIVB Volleyball Women's World Championship. At that moment it was as if a long-cherished dream was suddenly shattered.

The match stopped abruptly. The spectators who were passionately cheering for the Chinese team suddenly fell into silence. They could hardly accept this fact.

To many people's surprise, Lang Ping kept smiling instead of shedding tears despite being saddened by such a regrettable defeat.

Outside the stadium, it started to rain, adding to the chill of fall.

13.

At the night of losing to Italy, Lang Ping took a sleeping pill before going to bed.

After returning to the hotel from the fierce five-set match, she began discussing with Lai Yawen and An Jiajie about how to prepare for the third-place final against the Netherlands.

"We need to get our players out of the frustrating defeat as soon as possible. The bronze-medal match is also important. What we have achieved so far is based on our long-term efforts. We shall never give up even when we have no chance to compete for the championship," said Lang Ping.

After dinner, while the players were taking a bath, Lang Ping rested on the bed for a while, still holding the material of technical statistics of the match between China and Italy.

Upon receiving the call from Lai for discussing the arrangement of video study in the evening, Lang Ping went out of bed and turned on her computer. "I'll take the time to go over the video of the Netherlands again."

At the team meeting held in that evening, all players were quite depressed, feeling it rather a pity to lose the match, given so much effort that had been made. Lang Ping quite understood what they thought, but she was more aware of their responsibilities at this moment.

"Now that we have no chance to have our national anthem played, we should at least try our best to have our national flag raised." Lang Ping's words, full of power, were really inspiring.

Yan Ni, usually less talkative, stepped forward: "We performed better than what we had expected before the match. We should be fully prepared for tomorrow's competition!"

In the following morning, Lang Ping motivated her players again at the pre-match preparation meeting.

"Look, how downhearted you all are! You shouldn't slack off and must brace yourselves up!" Lang Ping tried to motivate their passion, "We don't aim at the gold medal only. Bronze medal also deserves our day-after-day efforts. In the past six months, you have been getting up at seven in the morning and training for seven or even eight hours, every day! What a pity it would be if you lose the momentum at the last minute!"

"We must win this bronze medal!"

At 4:40 p.m., October 20, Tokyo time, the Chinese team and the Dutch team appeared at the entrance for athletes.

The crowd was seething with excitement and many Chinese spectators in red clothes were quite conspicuous.

Hundreds of Chinese fans from all over China, together with over one thousand Chinese fans living in Japan, turned the Yokohama Stadium into the home turf of the Chinese team.

In the 22nd day of the FIVB Volleyball Women's World Championship, the top four teams began their 13th matches.

The schedule of matches was so tight that the dark circles under Zhu Ting's eyes were increasingly obvious. This resulted from her great pressure, heavy responsibility, being unaccustomed to local diets and insufficient sleep.

"This is the most difficult competition I've ever had during the six years since I joined the national team," said Zhu

At the 2018 FIVB Volleyball Women's World Championship, the Chinese women's volleyball team won a precious bronze medal after addressing great challenges by encouraging each other. (Photo by Li Zhiyan)

Ting. One of her friends tried to comfort her in this way: "You feel it difficult because you are so competent. The fact that you remain so competent even in such a challenging situation shows that you are stronger than before."

In this competition for the bronze medal, Zhu once again played a full match, maintaining full attendance of all 13 matches. She, as the outside hitter, assumed more responsibility of serve receiving. She had 9 kills in 18 attempts and had an ace.

With Zhu Ting's powerful serve receiving and strong support from back row, Li Yingying, who was among the starting lineup for the first time since the beginning of the World Championship, performed quite well in attacks. She was China's top scorer with 20 points including16 kills in 28 attempts plus 4 aces. Yuan Xinyue and Gong Xiangyu each scored 11 points, and the veteran player Yan Ni 9. In the last match of the World Championship, the Chinese team fulfilled their tactics of enabling players of various positions to score points.

When it came to the match point, Ding Xia passed the ball to Zhu Ting, who made a kill. Although it was rather a pity that the Chinese team failed to reach the final, it was also a kind of fulfillment as they completed their last match at the World Championship with a stunning victory.

It was for the first time that the Chinese players took off their protective gears with great ease during the six months after this Chinese team was established in 2018 and since the beginning of the World Championship. Their feelings at that moment were like that of students who were tidying up their schoolbags after their final exam.

No one could expect the challenges ahead. However, they supported and encouraged each other. It was their teamwork that helped them win this precious bronze medal.

14.

It was really a precious bronze medal for the Chinese team. Of the top three teams of that world championship, namely the U.S., China and Brazil, only China was the team seen on the victory podium again.

The Chinese team competed in four cities within 26 days. Led by Lang Ping, these Chinese players wrote a legend with their courage and persistence, which left an impressive and memorable mark in the history of Chinese volleyball.

"In the international volleyball community, there are so

Lang Ping deserved a thumbs-up for her team's bronze medal at the 2018 FIVB Volleyball Women's World Championship. (Photo by Shi Hui)

many world-class teams that are basically even in strength. The bronze medal didn't come easily, and it should be attributed to our joint efforts," said Lang Ping.

Lai Yawen joked: "This time it is not a silver medal. Bronze medal is good, as it is of the similar color as the gold medal."

Four years ago, when the Chinese team won a silver medal at the FIVB Volleyball Women's World Championship held in Italy for the second time in 16 years, Lai wrote a long post on her Weibo entitled "Our Silver World Championships" as follows:

"The 2014 FIVB Volleyball Women's World Championship is over. Coach Lang, this is your sixth World Championship over the past 32 years, and mine, too, over the past 24 years. At the 1990 FIVB Volleyball Women's

World Championship held in Beijing, you were the outside hitter of the team. At the age of 30, you were the eldest player of the team. Aged 20, I, the middle blocker, was the youngest player of the team. We cooperated so well that we won a silver medal. Eight years later, at the 1998 FIVB Volleyball Women's World Championship held in Japan, you, at the age of 38, became the head coach; I, aged 28, became the captain of the team. You gave instructions off the court, and I carried out your orders on the court. We worked together to win a silver medal. Sixteen years later, at the 2014 FIVB Volleyball Women's World Championship held in Japan, you, aged 54, were the head coach; and I, aged 44, was your assistant coach. Sitting side by side, you directed the players and I provided advice, which led our team to win a silver medal again. After winning the FIVB Volleyball Women's World Championship in 1982 and

During the FIVB Volleyball Women's World Championship, the fans group followed the Chinese women's volleyball team to various cities across China. (Photo by Li Zhiyan)

1986, we two worked together to reach the finals of the World Championship three times. However, every time there remained a little bit of regret for us. We have tried our best, and the regret embodies our long-term persistence in another way."

Lang Ping participated in the World Championships of 1982, 1986, 1990, 1998, 2006, 2014 and 2018, and Lai Yawen participated in the 1990, 1994, 1998, 2002, 2010, 2014 and 2018 World Championships. Putting these records together, it shows that they have participated in all the ten World Championships over the 36 years.

This time, they fulfilled their missions again.

Zhu Ting once said: "What is the ultimate goal of an athlete? I'm still looking for it. Today, we are returning in triumph."

"The Women's World Championship is just the beginning of a new cycle and our focus is on the matches in 2020." The above words by Lang Ping guided the Chinese players to look into the future.

CHAPTER SEVEN

2019

Having the national flag raised, and the national anthem played

When the sports competition season of the national team came to an end, Lang Ping began her "winter vacation". After an overuse for more than half a year, her replaced hips required a period of rehabilitation and treatment.

As soon as the surgery was completed in 2017, the doctor told her that the new joint prosthesis' service life would be up to 20 years. The doctor reiterated that the prosthesis must be taken good care of, otherwise Lang Ping would have to replace them again at the age of 80. This required her not to stand all day long on the court. However, she was too busy to attend to her health. It was only after all her players had returned to their respective provincial teams that she was aware of the acute discomfort of her joint prosthesis. She had to begin rehabilitation and receive treatments as soon as possible.

She assigned a lot of "homework" for her winter vacation. She required Yuan Lingxi to save on a hard disk the videos of all the important matches of the Chinese team in the previous year, and she planned to review all of them against her self-written documents.

She wanted to think through all the processes involved and take into account all factors, so as to figure out the best possible solutions and tactics.

Lang Ping always tried her best in every match. When she lost a competition, she would congratulate the opponent for their good performance in an elegant manner. At the same time she would made up her mind to win next time.

During her winter vacation, Lang Ping made a thorough analysis and summary of the factors that led to the failure of the Chinese team at the 2018 FIVB Volleyball Women's World Championship.

In 2018, the new Chinese team participated in the world-class matches for the first time after many veteran players had retired. The cooperation between the key players and other ones needed to be further improved. The ultimate failure of the Chinese team resulted from factors such as insufficient training time available for the team, weakness in the command of technical skills and the lack of attention to details.

This required the Chinese team to concentrate on their training.

Lang Ping, in particular, highlighted such words as "Pay special attention to details" in her notebook by circling them with a symbol of emphasis. She hoped that the next year all the players could meet the following requirements: to further fine-tune all details of their technical skills during training; to have a deeper insight into the opponent's skills; to pay special attention to all details during the competition.

In 2019, the top priority for the Chinese team was to gain access to the Tokyo Olympic Games as soon as possible.

1.

On March 12, 2019, the 500-day countdown to the Tokyo Olympic Games began.

In this day, the preparation for the match had been undergoing for 30 days in the volleyball hall of the Training Bureau of the General Administration of Sports of China. The big national team of China in 2019 recruited many young players born in the 2000s. Lang wanted to give volleyball players a platform to demonstrate their competence, so as to develop a bigger talent pool for the Tokyo and Paris Olympic Games and even further.

"Young players, you should never believe that you still enjoy age advantage. As you just joined the national team, you are definitely not eligible for the major matches of this or next year. Your capability will depend on the progress you make. Even if you have no chance to play in the major matches of this or next year, the Chinese team will need you in the near future. As long as you are in the national team, you must treat yourself as one of their members and devote yourself to training."

When talking to these young players under the age of 20, Lang Ping hoped that they would be professional volleyball players with full commitment.

Yang Hanyu was one of them.

As one of the key young players that the Chinese team focused on training for the Tokyo Olympic Cycle, Yang Hanyu was lucky enough to participate in the 2018 FIVB Volleyball Women's World Championship. Although the time of her playing in the match was rather limited, performing in such world-class matches made her further realize her own deficiencies and thus set up her clear goal. She really benefited a lot from this.

"In 2019, I hope I can step up my efforts to become a more capable player of this team."

Just three years ago, Yang Hanyu was watching live TV with her teammates of the junior team in a large conference room and played firecrackers to celebrate the victory of the Chinese team at the 2016 Rio Olympic Games. Thanks to the recruitment program advocated by the national team of China, Yang won the chance to compete in the Tokyo Olympic Games scheduled to be held 500 days later.

Yan Ni, who had just celebrated her 32nd birthday, was busy with packing up before returning to the national team.

Four and a half months ago, after the FIVB Volleyball Women's World Championship, Yan Ni had handed in the door card of the Athlete Apartments before she left Beijing. After the 2016 Rio Olympic Games, each time when the national team season of 2017 or 2018 was over, Yan Ni would say so when packing up her luggage before returning home: "I don't think I'll come back next year. I'm too old and I have so many sports injuries."

However, despite her memory of so many pains and sufferings, she was again ready to participate in the match together with these younger players who were born after 1995. Of course, sometimes she still said, "Young people are so energetic that I don't want to compete with them anymore."

In the same day, Liu Xiaotong, who just won the champion of the China Women Volleyball League, was scheduling to return to the national team after a two-day holiday.

In the previous year, Liu had a total of seven days off,

including the two days of holiday after the end of the China Women Volleyball League, a two-day holiday in Beijing, after returning from the FIVB Volleyball Women's World Championship and a three-day holiday for the whole team. Whenever she felt exhausted, Lang Ping's words would occur to her: "It is a kind of happiness that you are needed by others. It is of even greater happiness to be needed by your country."

On this day, as an NPC deputy, Zhang Changning was attending the NPC and CPPCC sessions. After the sessions, she would return to the national team.

"I hope I can make much more progress over the next 500 days!" Zhang Changning set a short-term goal for herself.

On this day, Ding Xia had her three wisdom teeth extracted, because she would have no time for taking care of her toothache afterwards.

On this day, Zhu Ting arrived in Moscow with VakifBank Istanbul team, preparing for the quarterfinal match of CEV Volleyball Champions League.

In 2019, a new slogan was put up in the Chinese team's training hall: Further enhance the sense of mission, responsibility and honor, and build a really competent national team.

The Chinese team set new goals for the next year.

2.

Since this year was critically important for preparing for the Olympic Games, Lang Ping told Lai Yawen that she wanted to invite Xu Yunli and Wei Qiuyue back to enhance the team's strength.

In the 40-year history of the Chinese women's volleyball team, it was not seldom the case that veteran players were invited back when the team needed them. The veteran players have played very important roles in the development of the Chinese team. After years of training, the spirit of the Chinese team has become an indispensable part of these Chinese players. They tried their best to make the spirit sustainable. It is the mission of Xu Yunli and Wei Qiuyue to pass such spirit on to the younger players.

After the 2016 Rio Olympic Games, Lang Ping had been considering the idea of retaining some veteran players. However, Hui Ruoqi was in poor health. Xu Yunli and Wei Qiuyue suffered so serious sports injuries that they had to undergo operations in 2017 and 2018 respectively. Therefore, they could only serve as "young assistant coaches", trying to help the team improve training results based on their own practical experiences and guide the young players on how to become the key players.

The participation of Xu Yunli added force to the group of middle blockers. Lai Yawen, Wu Xiaolei and Xu Yunli oversaw the training of Yan Ni, Yuan Xinyue, Wang Yuanyuan, Yang Hanyu, Hu Mingyuan and Zheng Yixin.

The three setters, Ding Xia, Yao Di and Diao Linyu, found it a good opportunity to get advice from Wei Qiuyue. Besides fine-tuning skills together, Wei often shared her practical experience on how to handle the ball when competing on the court.

Wei Qiuyue took part in the training camp in Zhangzhou in 2016. Three years later when she returned to Zhangzhou, she found the Athlete Apartment where they took photos was gone and was replaced by a new 12-storey building under construction. Fortunately, they had kept the photos which recorded the old days they spent here.

Over a dozen years with the Chinese team, Xu Yunli and Wei Qiuyue had gone through difficulties. Due to their perseverance and unyielding spirit, they fulfilled their dreams. This was fully demonstrated by their performance in the 2008 Beijing Olympic Games, the 2012 London Olympic Games and the 2016 Rio Olympic Games. This time they were recruited to the Chinese team again to help the young players better prepare for the 2020 Tokyo Olympic Games. They were expected to improve their young teammates' competency with their experience and conviction.

3.

The third professional season of Zhu Ting in Turkey was her last one there before temporarily leaving VakifBank Istanbul.

Zhu had already won seven champion titles within two and a half years, including two champions of CEV Volleyball Champions League and the FIVB Volleyball Women's World Cup each, as well as the trophies of the Turkish League, the Turkish Cup and the Turkish Super Cup each. In addition, she also won five MVP trophies and four awards of "Best Outside Spiker," an unprecedented achievement.

The Final of the Turkish Women's Volleyball League was the final chance for winning a champion title of the whole season. Again, VakifBank Istanbul met Eczacibasi, a well-known team with some of the best players in the world. VakifBank Istanbul lost the first set. After 2-2 tie in the first four sets, in the fifth set VakifBank Istanbul managed to win over Eczacibasi on the opponent's home turf.

With eight titles and six MVP trophies within three years, Zhu Ting returned to the China Women Volleyball League.

"The experience in Turkey was like a window for me to expand my horizon." This was Zhu's description of the volley competitions in Europe where she played for three years. Such valuable experiences were really important for Zhu to broaden her vision, enrich her experience and improve her ability. During the busiest months of competitions, the schedules were so tight that she had to take part in 8 matches within 24 days, which posed great challenges to her.

"Over the course of the three years, I can feel that I have become psychologically mature. I can better control myself both on the court and in life."

It was these three years that benefited Zhu Ting so much. However, after the Olympic year began, the excessive energy consumption of an athlete was more obvious due to the long span of the European League. In order to get down to the preparation of the Olympic year together with her teammates at an early date, Zhu decided to take a break from the European competition.

Zhu returned to China 85 days before the Olympic qualifying competition, which would begin in early August. Giovanni Guidetti would lead the Turkish Women's Volleyball Team to Beilun to compete with China, Germany and the Czech Republic for the qualification for the Tokyo Olympic Games.

"It couldn't have been arranged on purpose, right?" Zhu Ting said to herself.

By then, the Chinese women's volleyball team had mobilized their players for the matches of 2019. On the second day after Zhu Ting returned to Beijing, An Jiajie led a team mainly consisting of young players to Europe to compete in the Montreux Volley Masters. Then they flew to the South America to begin the first-stop match of the FIVB VNL that was held in Brasilia, the capital of Brazil.

Lang Ping led the team of major players to take part in the second-week competition of the FIVB VNL in Macau.

The 22 Chinese players were divided into two teams, and took turns to participate in the frequent matches. This was the new attempt made by Lang Ping, Lai Yawen and An Jiajie in 2019 based on their experience of the previous six years. As the Chinese team needed to both perform well in the matches and develop their talent pool, it was rather important to do more within limited time. According to the event schedule, they made a detailed plan and set the following targets:

To both fine-tune the starting lineup and train the young players; to both spend sufficient training time on honing skills and put aside enough time for rest; to both gain deeper insight into all the major opponents by playing with them and not to unveil the Chinese team's trump cards to them.

From the day of An Jiajie's departure, they found that it was really a tight and challenging schedule for all of them.

Lang Ping was responsible for the training of the starting lineup in Beijing. As soon as she got up early in the morning, she would first turn on her mobile phone to check if any message came from An Jiajie the night before. After hurriedly calling him for just few words, she had to hurry down to have breakfast before the morning training session.

While Montreux was at dawn, it was already in the

afternoon in Beijing. The two Chinese teams led by An Jiajie and Lang Ping were busy with the morning training in Switzerland and the afternoon training in Beijing respectively. When Coach An completed his daily tasks, Lang Ping was very sleepy as it was already late at night in Beijing. She tried to refresh herself and organized a telephone meeting for communicating and discussing about the matches and personnel arrangement. During this period, each day the meeting didn't end until the midnight Beijing time.

After the Montreux Volley Masters was over, Coach An and his team flew to Brazil for new competitions, and Lai Yawen departed from Beijing to meet them in Brazil. Lang Ping, who remained in Beijing, had to switch to the "South American channel": the time difference between them increased from seven hours to ten hours. Their days and nights were almost reversed.

They tried to provide the limited opportunities of real competitions to these young players whose skills needed to be improved. They needed to make adjustment after communication according to the problems identified in competitions. They needed to try their best to improve the players' technical skill and help the team make continuous progress along with each match. In most cases, as soon as finishing the online meeting with Lang Ping, Lai Yawen and An Jiajie would either communicate with their players to inspire their morale or guide them on further study of or preparation for the competitions. The FIVB VNL, however, only held three matches a week. The matches were over when Lang Ping, Lai Yawen and An Jiajie managed to get familiar with the time difference and the event schedule.

For the 22 members of the Chinese team, this process was like a long-distance race. Everyone was working in the same direction, but no one knew who would finally succeed and who would fail. Whatever difficulties they were facing, they had no choice but to hang on and forge ahead.

4.

The third-week competitions of the FIVB VNL were held in Hong Kong, where China met Italy that had scored one victory after another in Europe.

Both Lang Ping and Italy's coach Davide Mazzanti attached great importance to the strategic significance of the match. Italy wanted to continue their winning streak, while China certainly didn't want to lose the match.

Italy didn't send all members of their starting lineup during the first eight rounds of the FIVB VNL. To win this match with China, Mazzanti sent all the major players on to the court during this match.

The starting lineup of the Chinese team for this match were all members of the team winning the Olympic champion: The outside hitters Zhu Ting and Zhang Changning, the middle blockers Yuan Xinyue and Yan Ni, the opposite hitter Gong Xiangyu, the setter Ding Xia, and the libero Lin Li. Except Lin Li, the libero of the Chinese team, the other 13 members on the starting lineup sheets of both teams were the same as the that of the two teams that participated in the semi-finals of the 2018 FIVB Volleyball Women's World Championship.

From the beginning of the match, Italy suppressed China with powerful serving and quick attack. This helped them gain a leading score. Under the heavy serves by Egonu, the Chinese team's performance in serve receiving was rather poor. The on-site knotmeter showed that the speed of her ace reached 101.5 km/h. The Chinese team stuck in rotation not long after the beginning of the match, which quickly extended the lead of Italy. The Chinese team lost the first two sets with 18-25 and 22-25 almost the same as what happened in 2018.

The unyielding spirit demonstrated by the Chinese players in the difficult situation reminds us of Lang Ping's classic interpretation of the spirit of the Chinese women's volleyball team: The essence of the Chinese team's spirit is not about winning the championship, but to always try their best in trials and tribulations though sometimes it was impossible to win.

In the third set, Lang sent Li Yingying and Zhu Ting as the outside hitters in starting lineup, Liu Xiaotong still as the opposite hitter, and Wang Mengjie replacing Lin Li as the libero. On the bench, other Chinese players including Zhang Changning, Zeng Chunlei and Hu Mingyuan, etc., were warming up and waiting for instructions from the coach team.

The Chinese team lagged behind for most of the third set before it tied the score 22-22 near the end of the set. When it was the turn of Egonu to serve again, Lang Ping requested substitution again!

The ball served by Egonu was still so powerful that the Chinese player had to directly dig the ball over net, which allowed the opponent to organize one fiercer counterattack. Li Yingying reacted so quickly that she timely defended the ball and organized an attack in a hurry. The spike by Zhu Ting on zone 2 was blocked by the opponent and Wang Mengjie succeeded in helping defend the ball! Then Liu Xiaotong dug the ball for Zhu Ting who successfully made a powerful spike. 23-22!

This hard-won point moved Yuan Xinyue, who was sitting

on the bench, into tears. Her facial expression indicated, "Great!"

When the Chinese team had the set point of the third set, the Italians requested timeout.

Hu Mingyuan was just about to run over to her teammates to hand them towels and water when she saw Lang Ping gesture to her, "Get ready to serve." She quickly warmed up by running around the warm-up area and moving her arms, exactly as she did in the semi-finals of the FIVB Volleyball Women's World Championship. It was time to test if she, a middle blocker, was capable of fulfilling such a monumental task.

Hu Mingyuan had been entrusted by Lang Ping to serve at critical moments during the FIVB Volleyball Women's World Championship. This time she was ordered to serve at the end of the set.

"I didn't think of anything but the action tips of how to serve." Hu Mingyuan again served a good ball before an Italian player directly dug the ball high up to Egonu who confidently took off, swung her arm and spiked. Across the net, two-meter-tall Yuan Xinyue jumped with full force after adjusting her paces. Her timely blocking defended the heavy spike by Egonu from a perfect angle. When the ball was grounded on the playing court, Yuan Xinyue screamed loudly with her own sound effects, "Great!"

The Chinese team won the third set 25-23. Although it was just one set back, the Chinese players and the Chinese spectators were as happy as if they had won the match.

In the fourth set, Egonu's serving was still so powerful that every time her serve round, almost four Chinese players worked together to receive the serve. Then they organized an effective attack while strengthening blocking and defence and patiently looking for opportunities.

After a 24-24 tie at the end of the set, Zhu Ting scored a point with a power attack. Then Egonu stepped on the line when making back-row attack. Lai Yawen, who was sitting in the coach bench, jumped up excitedly and indicated to the referee with her finger towards the opponent's three-meter line. Lai, a veteran who experienced the turnaround in the competition between China and Russia at the 2004 Athens Olympic Games and the cut-throat match between China and Brazil at the Rio Olympic Games, seldom betrayed her feelings like this. Her unusual reaction showed that the competition was so fierce and it was so difficult for the Chinese team to embrace a turnaround under such an unfavorable situation.

China won the fourth set 26-24, tying the score at 2-2.

It was a five-set match.

At the end of this set, Italy overtook with 13-11. At this critical moment, Zhu Ting took her turn to serve. It turned out to be an ace. Then Zhu broke the opponents' serve receiving, which allowed Li Yingying to block directly the spike by Egonu. On match point, Zhu Ting served and Egonu spiked the ball out of the court. The Italian was not willing to accept their failure and challenged the call. However, the official review showed that the ball did go out of the baseline.

15-13! The Chinese team won the fifth set and won the match 3-2!

In the unfavorable condition, the Chinese team, with the spirit of never giving up, achieved a near-miraculous turnaround in their competition with the powerful opponent. When the Chinese team sealed the victory, the Chinese players formed a circle in the middle of the court, jumping and circling...

In the third year of preparation for the Tokyo Olympic Games, the young Chinese players, with their tenacious efforts and excellent teamwork, achieved a big reversal in the competition with Italy, their most formidable opponent over the previous three years. This once again proved that the Chinese team were definitely the most capable team, if not the strongest!

5.

A month later, the somewhat proud Italians came to China to "take revenge."

The finals were held in Nanjing, China. However, since the finals were followed by the Olympic qualifying tournament only three weeks later, all teams had their respective concerns for their own interests.

Serbia, which rose to No. 1 in the world rankings by FIVB after winning the FIVB Volleyball Women's World Championship, gave up the chance to enter the finals out of strategic considerations. As the Chinese team ranked No. 1 in the sub-tournament and were the host, they definitely had to participate in the finals. However, after deliberation, the coach decided to challenge other volleyball powerhouses with a team of young players led by An Jiajie, the assistant coach.

To the surprise of all, Italian team sent a team of all their major players to Nanjing. It was said that Italian players came to take revenge for their defeat by China with 2-3 at the match in Hong Kong. If Italian team missed this opportunity, there would be no chance for them to compete against their Chinese counterpart in 2019. If so, these condescending

Italian players could hardly accept it.

At the press conference before the finals, both the Chinese coaches and players were young ones, which caused the dissatisfaction of other teams, especially America and Italy. What made the Chinese team, with the absence of their eight major players, occupy a seat in the finals? What competitiveness could be expected for this new team?

On the first match day, China was outplayed by Turkey 1-3, which further lowered the expectations of the Chinese team. Many Chinese fans began to change their flights and claim refunds for their hotel reservations, planning to take the night train home after watching the match of group stage.

Compared with Zhu Ting, Yuan Xinyue and Zhang Changning that enjoyed outstanding capabilities in all aspects, the 14 young Chinese players attending the finals were not favored. The news that the Chinese team didn't send their major players to the finals caused violent reactions of all parties concerned. However, these young players really cherished this opportunity to play in such important matches.

In their competition with China, Italy fielded their strongest squad, except for Sylla who went to hospital on sick leave. The starting lineup of the Chinese team included the outside hitters Liu Xiaotong and Liu Yanhan, the middle blockers Wang Yuanyuan and Zheng Yixin, the opposite hitter Gong Xiangyu, the setter Yao Di and the libero Ni Feifan.

The Chinese team strictly followed their tactics plan from serving part. In the first half of the set, the practice of continuously serving towards the young outside hitter Petrini as the target proved quite effective. This resulted in the opponent's continuous poor or even failed serve receiving. China took 8-4 lead into the first technical timeout.

Except for the powerful spikes by Egonu, most of the attacks by other Italian team members were effectively defended or saved by the Chinese players who then organized excellent counterattack. The proud Italian players never expected to play so laboriously with China's substitutes. Being increasingly impatient, they frequently made mistakes. On the contrary, the Chinese team had been maintaining advantage and won the first set 25-17 smoothly.

As the youngest player on the Chinese team's lineup sheet in 2019, the 18-year-old Ni Feifan met Egonu across the net for the first time. Prior to that, as for the kind of balls served by Egonu with a speed up to more than 100 km/h, Ni had only received them from the serving machine. Instead of being afraid of such high-speed balls, she even had an urge to try them.

In the second set, after withstanding the aggressive attack from the opponent, the Chinese team found the chance for counterattack when the two teams tied 15-15!

When it was Gong Xiangyu's turn to serve, the Chinese team scored four points in a row to surpass with 19-15. After the Italian team were closing the gap, Liu Yanhan scored four points in a row with her powerful attacks. Then, with the successful counterattack by Gong Xiangyu, China won the second set 25-22.

It was a fantastic start that the Chinese team did not dare to anticipate before the match.

After being pulled back a set by the Italian team, the Chinese players hugged and encouraged each other in the fourth set for every wonderful rally they won.

"Hold on! Don't let up! Never doubt yourself!"

At the mid of the set, Liu Yanhan, who had been playing

very smoothly, was suddenly hampered in her attack. Coach An Jiajie took Liu Yanhan off the court to have a rest. When standing on the bench, she tried to pep herself up, "We must hold on to the end."

At the key point at the end of the set, An Jiajie sent Liu Yanhan onto the court again. Liu Xiaotong hugged her and cheered her on. "You are playing very well! Don't worry! I'll give you good protection!"

It was with the two points scored in a row by the cool-headed Liu Yanhan that China got the match point at 24-21. The last point was scored by the middle blocker Wang Yuanyuan. At the very moment of the ball's being grounded on the court, the Chinese girls were so excited that they raised their arms and cheered.

Just as what they did a month ago, these underestimated girls also gathered in a group, raising their hands high into the air, expressing their lofty sentiments.

6.

The moment she won the match, Gong Xiangyu burst into tears.

The last time she shed tears on the court was in the 2016 Rio Olympic Games after the semi-finals victory over the Netherlands. In the previous three years, under the pressure of being famous at a young age, Gong Xiangyu still worked very hard in a down-to-earth and steady manner, endeavoring to develop herself into the one most needed by the Chinese team.

"At that moment, I realized that our team of players that

attended this match were probably not among the best ones, but we were no doubt among the most hardworking ones." Gong said.

Shedding tears was really a good way of releasing her emotions.

In the match between China and Italy held in Hong Kong, Gong Xiangyu was one of the seven-member starting lineup, but was also the only one that wasn't sent back onto the playing court after being substituted. Before the match with Italy in Nanjing, she changed her usual style of speech. "Be more aggressive. Never give up!"

It is said that the Chinese team are one of the best teams enjoying the highest morale, which has become an indispensable part of every member of the team.

Motivated by this victory, these young underdogs before the match went on to outplay Turkey 3-1 in the competition for the third place. Despite the fact that they weren't given enough attention from the beginning, they forged ahead until they climbed to the podium of the finals. The previous challenges had become their valuable experience and ultimately their persistence paid off.

Seeing Liu Yanhan be awarded "Best Outside Spiker," Liu Xiaotong recalled what she had been through five years ago. Five years later, also at the finals of the FIVB World Grand Prix, also playing with the starting lineup of substitutes, Liu Yanhan finally won the award of "Best Outside Spiker," which further improved her confidence towards the established goal.

It was also the goal of Zheng Yixin, a girl from Zhangzhou, Fujian Province, to become the "most needed one" of the Chinese team at an early date.

In 2015, she was selected for the first time into the Chinese team. During the preparation for the 2016 Rio Olympic Games, she participated in competitions on behalf of the national team for several times. However, she didn't become the key players of the national team. Before leaving for the finals, Coach An told Zheng, "This is an opportunity for you. But it favors you only when you manage to seize it on the court." In such a team that was underestimated, Zheng Yixin finally "freed" her mind, "Only by giving full play to the potential of each individual can the collective power get stronger."

On her way from Nanjing to Beilun by train to join the main Chinese team, Liu Yanhan was deep in thought while looking out of the window at the blue sky, rice fields and distant mountains. "Next, I will try to keep on such good feeling."

No one could have expected that in 2019 it was Italy team, China's most formidable opponent, who boosted the morale of the Chinese team. It was the real progress made by these underestimated young players that gave the Chinese team enough confidence to compete with other powerhouses.

7.

Early in the morning on August 4, 2019, Zhu Ting was awakened by the alarm. After getting up, she glanced at her phone and muttered to herself. "Countdown zero to the match day. It finally comes!"

On this day, the Chinese team would compete with the Turkish team in the Olympic qualification match. It was the most important task this year for the Chinese team to win the access to the Tokyo Olympic Games by upsetting Turkey. In order to ensure the access to the Games at an early time, the major players of the Chinese team carried out the training camp in Beilun for six weeks, where they trained from dawn to night and the life was monotonous and dull. The clock was ticking in everyone's mind.

"It feels like a student preparing for the National College Entrance Examination." Zhu Ting made such an analogy.

This match was the sixth one between China and Turkey within less than a year.

After Zhu Ting joined the Turkish club VakifBank Istanbul three years ago, the Turkey-China competitions always attracted special attention. Seeing the powerful Zhu Ting standing across the net, the Turkish coach Giovanni Guidetti and a number of Turkey's national players playing for VakifBank Istanbul somewhat felt less confident before the competition. As this match was of critical importance, it was the common concern for both Chinese fans and Guidetti to know how Lang Ping would use Zhu Ting in the match.

In the first seven months of 2019, the two teams met four times, in which Lang only sent most of the major players to play with Turkey once in their match of the FIVB VNL in Jiangmen, and in this match, Zhu played for five minutes and had 2 kills in three attempts.

"Zhu Ting won't be among the starting lineup," Lang Ping announced at a preparation meeting before the Jiangmen match, "Everyone on the court must try to fulfill her duty and deliver her best performance." Zhang Changning immediately understood what Lang meant. If the Chinese team could still win the match with Turkey even in the absence of Zhu Ting, they would enjoy psychological advantages in the following competition for the access to the Olympic Games.

In that match, the Chinese team only encountered challenges at the end of the first set. When the Chinese team lagged behind the opponent 23-24, Lang Ping sent Zhu Ting into the court. Zhu made two heavy spikes, one of which saved the set point and the other sealed the victory. After the 0-3 defeat to the Chinese team, Giovanni Guidetti, who was on the bench, said resentfully, "Because Zhu Ting was not on our side."

The Turkish team arrived in Beilun several days before this Olympic qualification match. However, during the player qualification review, it was suddenly learned that Turkey's outside hitter Meliha could not participate. When answering the media's questions about the impact of Meliha's absence, Guidetti said childishly, "The key is that we don't have Zhu Ting."

Despite the compliments by the opponent, Zhu Ting stayed focused all the time. "We have been fully prepared for the match. Everyone in our team is quite familiar with the characteristics and habits of every member in the Turkish team."

During the pre-match warm-up on the court, Zhu Ting noticed the opponent's young middle blocker Zehra Gunes looking at her. Zehra was the teammate of Zhu Ting at VakifBank Istanbul. Usually, players didn't communicate with each other through facial expressions before a match, but this time Zhu smiled at Zehra.

The Chinese team showed that they were extremely well prepared from the very beginning of the match, suppressing the opponent in all aspects. All the opponent's changes were expected by the Chinese team.

Zhang Changning consecutively scored in attack and blocking. This helped the Chinese team enter the first technical timeout with 8-5. When Zhu Ting attacked from the front row, her powerful spikes of wide variety were too powerful for the opponent.

When leading with 20-16, Gong Xiangyu struggled to save a dink spike by the opponent. As it was too late for Yan Ni to react, she barely dug the ball to the position 4 behind Zhu Ting, a place about five meters from the net. Under normal circumstances such a ball had to be directly hit back over the net. Unexpectedly, Zhu Ting quickly stepped back and leaped up, leaned back and made a heavy spike. The ball was finally grounded on the opponent's court. This dominating spike threw the whole stadium into thundering of joy. Then the Chinese team scored several points consecutively and won this set with 25-18.

Seeing that the situation was not favorable, in the second set the Turkish team took the initiative to seek changes in their tactics. However, the Chinese team continued to control the situation and won this set 25-12.

Two sets ahead, Lang reminded her players to stay alert. She said loudly to the girls, "Let's start from zero!"

The third set was tied at 8-8, and then the Chinese team gradually took the initiative after the mid of the set, finally winning 25-18 and outplaying Turkey 3-0. It became the third team to gain access to the Tokyo Olympic Games after Japan and Brazil.

In the whole match, the Chinese team did not request any substitution. All the seven starting players performed and cooperated with each other very well. It seemed that the Turkish team were convinced of the result. When the two teams lined up to shake hands with each other after the match, the young player Zehra Gunes smilingly blew Zhu Ting a kiss. Although disappointed, Giovanni Guidetti stood near the referee's stand waiting for Zhu Ting and immediately had a smile on his face as the two came in for a big hug. At the post-match press conference, Guidetti spoke highly of Zhu Ting and Lang Ping, "If I had to choose, China would be the last opponent I want to meet. They have the best head coach in the world."

The Tokyo Olympic Organizing Committee prepared a Dharma doll, a symbol of good luck, for each team that will play in the Olympic Games. When the FIVB officials handed the dolls to the head coach Lang Ping and the captain Zhu Ting, the Chinese girls shouted together, "Tokyo, here we come!"

When they returned to the hotel, Lang Ping quickly packed up a thick pile of documents on the table. "Now I can finally dispose of them as the competition with Tukey is over this year. The most important task of 2019 is ultimately accomplished!" After packing up, Lang Ping and her players left for Beijing.

There was one last task for 2019—the FIVB Volleyball Women's World Cup in Japan.

8.

Four years later, the Chinese women's volleyball team were once again going to the FIVB Volleyball Women's World Cup.

All the way from Beijing to Tokyo, Lang Ping and the players could always hear the cheering of their compatriots for their team wherever they were. This was really a valuable asset accumulated through their solid efforts and remarkable achievements in the previous four years.

When waiting for luggage at Tokyo Haneda Airport, Zeng Chunlei, who was once appointed to take up the important role as captain at a critical moment, thought of the scene four years ago in the same place where the photo was taken. While considering "yesterday once more," Zeng Chunlei saw Li Yingying by her side. Putting her arm around Li, Zeng said, "This year I take photos with my younger sister. Four years later, my younger sister will take photos with her younger sister."

"Xiangyu, after a while, you push the first luggage cart and take the lead," coach Lai said to Gong.

"Okay! I'm glad to do that," said Gong Xiangyu, who had become one of the major players of the Chinese team, no longer the junior player of the youth team of Jiangsu province four years ago.

Four years ago, the bus dispatched by the organizing committee of the 2015 FIVB Volleyball Women's World Cup for picking up the Chinese team was parked in the outermost lane of the bus. The Chinese team boarded the bus that drove from Haneda Airport to Matsumoto, the venue for the first leg of the 2015 FIVB Volleyball Women's World Cup. This time, the team's bus started slowly from the same lane again and set off.

It was in Shin-Yokohama that the Chinese team completed their journey in the 2018 Volleyball Women's World Championship. A year later, the team began their competition in the FIVB Volleyball Women's World Cup from Shin-Yokohama. Seeing the same hotel and the gym again, the girls recalled their memory of the old days here.

"The scenes of our semi-finals against Italy and the

third-place finals against the Netherlands last year are still fresh in my mind. I can even recall the sound of the venue at that time," said Li Yingying.

"Coming to Yokohama again, I feel time goes by too fast. A year has passed," said Wang Mengjie.

Zhu Ting was more impressed by the words from Lang Ping here than the stadium itself. "When we failed to make it to the finals, Coach Lang inspired us. We were really motivated by her words 'Though we can't have our national anthem played, we must try to have our national flag raised.' It's really inspiring for us!"

In their first match of the FIVB Volleyball Women's World Cup on September 14, the Chinese team earned a landslide 3-0 victory over South Korea.

Lang Ping received interviews after the match. When speaking of her playing for the national team in the international arena from the age of 18, she was full of pride. "As long as you wear the jersey with 'China' on it, you are playing for China. Our goal in every match is to have the national flag raised or the national anthem played!"

Along with Lang Ping's highly recognized voice, such remarks as "Have the national flag raised or the national anthem played" became quite popular in China. On the eve of the 70th anniversary of the founding of the People's Republic of China, the Chinese people praised the Chinese women's volleyball team for their victory and were so greatly encouraged by such moving and confident words that these words became one of the most popular searches on the Internet.

9.

The Japanese were really good at collecting information. They came up with an information sheet covering the 49-year history of the volleyball matches between China and Japan for the newsroom.

This encounter between China and Japan in the FIVB Volleyball Women's World Cup on September 19, 2019, was the 199th competition between the two teams in 49 years since the 1970 Bangkok Asian Games on December 12, 1970. Of the 198 previous ones, China won 155 times and lost 43, holding an absolute advantage.

In the years of exchanges, interactions and competitions concerning volleyball between Chinese and Japanese volleyball communities, Lang Ping was one of the iconic figures of China volleyball. Many ordinary Japanese could recognize Lang Ping by calling her name in Japanese when meeting her on the street. As Lang Ping had numerous visits to Japan over these years, she gradually understood they were calling her name in Japanese.

Before every major volleyball match, Japanese reporters always asked Lang Ping some questions such as her comments on the Japanese team and the stories that happened between the Chinese team and Japanese team.

Before the match between the two teams at the FIVB Volleyball Women's World Cup, a Japanese reporter asked Lang Ping what she thought of the Japanese team, the long-term opponent of China. Lang Ping gave an insightful answer.

"In the history of Chinese women's volleyball, Japan

has given us much help. In the 1960s, Premier Zhou Enlai invited Coach Daimatsu Hirofumi to China to teach us volleyball. Every match we played with the Japanese team was a fierce competition and a rare opportunity for exchanging ideas. We learn from each other and improve together."

On the day of the match, the Chinese and Japanese teams appeared together, arousing enthusiastic atmosphere across the whole Yokohama Stadium. The fans of the Japanese team were numerous and imposing. A large number of Chinese living in Japan and Chinese fans who came all the way to watch the match also had enough enthusiasm to support the Chinese team. The Japanese fans in jerseys of "red and white" and the Chinese fans in "red and yellow" decorated the entire stadium into an enthusiastic "red sea".

Four years ago, the Chinese team won their first world champion title after defeating Japan in their last match of the FIVB Volleyball Women's World Cup.

"You will become the champion if you can upset Japan, but Japan won't let you get through this easily. You must fight for it by yourselves. At that time, these players were still young, didn't experience such kind of situation, and didn't have solid technical skills as they do now. Though we provided them with detailed guidance before the match, they still failed to perform as well as expected on the court. As they couldn't properly control themselves, even the balls served by them flew far away from the court. Now it's different. When I send them onto the court, I can see that they are self-assured and poised. They know where the pressure is and how to convert pressure into motivation, and how to control themselves." When speaking of the growth of her young players, Lang Ping, though tired, had a big grin on her face.

Thanks to the long-term systematic training, the Chinese team achieved great progress. In fact, they were still not the most powerful, fastest or the most aggressive team in the world. However, they became one of the most stable and united team with the greatest potential. These Chinese players, based on their diligence and hard work, combined with thorough study and careful preparation, gradually learned to have a deeper insight into themselves and competitions. They were capable of earning some landslide victories and upsetting powerful opponents.

For the Chinese team, the victory over their Japanese counterpart at this FIVB Volleyball Women's World Cup was one of the most sweeping ones in the competitions between the two teams both with starting lineup.

China's starting lineup of seven members had been performing and cooperating quite well from the Olympic qualification tournament with Turkey, to the match with Russia during the third-round stage at the FIVB Volleyball Women's World Cup, and to this match with Japan. Lang Ping once again used the starting lineup throughout the whole match without substitution.

"It is not worth being happy if you have a nice shot. Maybe the opponent will defend and strike it back. As long as the ball isn't grounded on the court, you should always pay full attention. Victory means that we need to win a match instead of just one set, and win the finals of an event instead of just one match!" During the competitions from Yokohama to Sapporo, Lang Ping always said so to her players.

10.

On September 23, 2017, it was a stormy day under typhoon No. 17 in Sapporo.

On the seventh match day of the 2019 FIVB Volleyball Women's World Cup, the Chinese women's volleyball team met the U.S. team, their long-term strong opponent. Although the Chinese players won all the previous matches with good performance, they felt that the real test didn't come until they met the U.S. team.

It was really difficult to deal with the U.S. team.

At the 2018 FIVB Volleyball Women's World Championship, China managed to outplay the U.S. for the first time in the world-class competitions over the previous several years. This helped China find out the way to deal with the U.S. team. However, the U.S. team, with stronger talent reserve, reshuffled their starting lineup in their training camp in 2019. Except for the two outside hitters, all other five members were changed.

It was this new U.S. team that upset their Chinese counterpart with starting lineup of major players 3-0 at the FIVB VNL in Jiangmen. Then they won the Chinese team consisting of younger players again 3-1 in the finals in Nanjing. The U.S. team were so powerful that they still could defend their title with their lineup mainly of new players.

After the FIVB VNL, Lang Ping joked when talking about the new situations of the following competitions between China and the U.S., "We have no choice but go on studying and make progress every day."

When drafting the competition plan, Lang underlined the words "Forge ahead in spite of difficulties." She demanded that all players should have a sense of mission when serving, "When serving, consider more for your teammates. If your serve is not good enough, your teammates will have to block or defend the opponent's attack with more efforts!"

In addition to "forging ahead in spite of difficulties,"

Lang Ping also always emphasized the importance of being "both smart and brave." Lai Yawen explained it at the preparation meeting, "The braver one of two powerful teams will win the match; the smarter one of two brave teams will win the match."

Compared with that a year ago at the FIVB Volleyball Women's World Championship, the starting lineup of the Chinese team remained unchanged. By contrast, except for the captain Jordan Larson, and Kelsey Robinson who had changed from the libero back to the outside hitter, all the other positions of the U.S. team were occupied by new players: the middle blockers Haleigh Washington and Chiaka Ogbogu, the opposite hitter Andrea Drews, the setter Jordyn Poulter and the libero Megan Courtney.

At the beginning, the Chinese team tried to suppress the opponent's speed by continuously serving with the libero Megan Courtney as the target. Each Chinese player faithfully implemented the tactics as required by the coach and kept on exerting pressure on the opponent with high-quality serves. This effectively prevented the U.S. team, known for their high speed, from organizing aggressive attacks.

In the first half of this set, though the U.S. coach Karch Kiraly consecutively requested two timeouts, they still didn't reverse the situation. After the second timeout, Yuan Xinyue consecutively grabbed the opportunities of counterattacks and direct spikes. China led 18-9 and further won the set 25-16.

The U.S. team didn't expect they would lose the first set by a large margin. Early in the second set, the U.S. team continuously lost the rallies for touching the net or passing the center line. For a strong team like the U.S. team, such performance only showed that they were "in a troubled mood."

Zhang Changning (top left), Yuan Xinyue (top right), Yan Ni (bottom left) and Zhu Ting (bottom right) are competing on the fields.
(Photo by Li Zhiyan)

As the unstable serve receiving undermined the teamwork of the United States, in many cases the U.S. players had to carry out attacks mainly based on individual strength. This allowed China to score quite some points through blocking. Though Kiraly was forced to reshuffle the lineup in the second half, it was too late as the Chinese team had widen their lead and won the second set 25-17.

After winning two sets, Coach Lang reminded her players to stay focused and continue to exert pressure on their opponents.

As expected, the U.S. team dramatically changed their lineup in the third set, which helped them somewhat pick up their momentum. After the score was tied at 7-7, the Chinese team managed to limit Lowe's attacks and scored 5 points in a row. Seeing the momentum would be gone, Kiraly continued to request substitutions. At the end of this set, the U.S. team once narrowed down the score difference to only one point. At this critical moment, Zhu Ting helped the Chinese team gain the match point with a powerful back-row attack. With the point scored by Zhang Changning's attack, the Chinese team won the third set 25-22.

In this fierce competition with the U.S. team, the most important one for the Chinese team during the FIVB Volleyball Women's World Cup, the Chinese team upset their counterpart 3-0. Both the process and the result were amazing. However, one would realize it was "the hard work that paid off" after reviewing the efforts and progress made by the Chinese team over the previous six months.

The match statistics showed that the Chinese team enjoyed an overall advantage over their American counterpart in all aspects. The captain Zhu Ting scored 23 points, followed by Zhang Changning, Yuan Xinyue and Gong Xiangyu, with 13, 10 and 6 points respectively. The above major players that emerged during the preparation for the 2016 Rio Olympic Games became the starting lineup of the Chinese team. This allowed the Chinese team to be really capable of competing against the world-class teams.

11.

Osaka is a blessed place for the Chinese women's volleyball team.

Lang Ping was in a good mood when she arrived in Osaka with eight consecutive wins. She thought of her first world campaign with the Chinese team 38 years ago in Osaka, where she won the championship trophy. As an athlete, Lang Ping and her teammates started their legend from Osaka.

The 1998 FIVB Volleyball Women's World Championship was the last world event coached by Lang Ping as the head coach of the Chinese team for the first time. She always made it her goal to reach the finals in Osaka.

In 2003, the Chinese team of the "Golden Generation" led by Chen Zhonghe regained the world title after 17 years. The competitions of the final stage were held in Osaka.

In the 2018 Volleyball Women's World Championship, the Chinese team arrived in Osaka for the most challenging competition of next stage. Their prospect suddenly became promising after they chalked up a quick win of 3-0 over the U.S. team.

Lang Ping once said in her autobiography *Legends of the Youth* that she enjoyed peace of mind whenever she came to Osaka for competition.

In the first match day of Osaka, China outplayed the Netherlands 3-1. If they could win Serbia, their 10th opponent of the event, they would win the championship one round in advance. No one had dared to expect such a favorable situation when the team went to the FIVB Volleyball Women's World Cup.

This day really came.

Almost all the Chinese fans who came to the scene to watch the match had a five-starred red flag in their hands. They all came with the hope that the Chinese team would win the 10th victory of world-class competitions on the occasion of the 70th anniversary of the founding of the People's Republic of China. Some of the fans were middle-aged and elderly people, the fans of the Chinese team of "elder generation".

"I have been the fans of the Chinese team for most of my life. When I was young, I couldn't afford to watch the match at the scene. Now I want to seize this opportunity to see Lang Ping commanding at the scene!" A fan in his 50s said from the bottom of his heart, and several people around him were moved into tears.

In sharp contrast to the enthusiasm of the outside world, the Chinese team completely focused on playing well every match in a stable and calm manner. Lang Ping made the following requirements for the players before the match: no arrogance, no impatience, no looseness and no nervousness.

As expected, China upset Serbia 3-0, thus winning the title of the FIVB Volleyball Women's World Cup one round in advance. The fans and media at the scene got ready to celebrate the victory together with the Chinese team. However, the expected scene never happened. After the match, these Chinese players were performing stretching exercises on the court as usual before leaving the court in a hurry. They showed no sign of ecstasy for winning the title in advance. After searching around the stadium, the reporters finally found the Chinese players in the physical training room.

After the victory, they were still undergoing their physical training as scheduled.

On the last match day, the Chinese team played against Argentina. Before the match, Lang Ping told the players, “Never forget the original aspiration and carry it through to the end.”

Wearing the jersey with “China” printed on the chest, one should devote herself to the mission and cause of the Chinese team. This was the original aspiration of the Chinese team. From the first day the team were formed, the Chinese team led by Lang Ping had been fulfilling their tasks day by day and never gave up when facing challenges. It was the same case in the 2015 Asian Women’s Volleyball Championship when the Chinese team fell into low tide period, or after the Chinese team won the 2015 FIVB Volleyball Women’s World Cup, or during the tough process of winning

China’s national flag and national anthem, the driving force behind the Chinese women’s volleyball team, inspired them to address challenges one after another and ultimately achieve excellence again. (Photo by Li Zhiyan)

the championship of the 2016 Rio Olympic Games, or again embarking on the preparation for the Tokyo Olympic Games.

"We have been following the principle of making stable and constant progress and accumulation on a daily basis since the 2019 training camp. Even during the most difficult times, we managed to achieve the goals set at the beginning of the year based on our teamwork."

After the Chinese team had defended their championship with eleven consecutive victories at the FIVB Volleyball Women's World Cup, Lang Ping said, "We never forget our original aspiration and carry it through to the end. As we just win the victory in this stage, our goal is still far from being achieved."

"Carrying the goal through to the end" was not only the expectation and requirements by Lang Ping for the Chinese team this time, but also a heartfelt statement to herself.

After coaching the Chinese team for the second time in 2013, she struggled to lead the Chinese team consisting of players younger than her daughter to return to the glory again. Even she did not expect that it took two Olympic preparation cycles for her to achieve this goal.

Lang Ping worked very hard under so heavy workload that even young people couldn't endure. Every day, she had to stand with the young players on the court for eight hours. In the evening she also needed to organize study for the players. "Even I, an old lady of nearly sixty, can do it. Who dare not work hard?"

Lang Ping often said so.

"I was really exhausted this year," Lang once said in private, "There are times when I am so tired that I want to cry. Maybe I'm really old." But on the volleyball court, Lang Ping was always in high spirits and high morale.

Within the seven years, Lang Ping, the "Iron Hammer," led the young Chinese team to go through various difficulties and challenges and continuously made progress and achieved glories.

The Chinese team won the champion of the FIVB Volleyball Women's World Cup with eleven consecutive victories, drawing wide attention around China.

It happened to be on the eve of the 70th anniversary of the founding of the People's Republic of China. The Chinese players were seen on the victory podium together with a specially prepared banner. The 31 Chinese members that participated in the 2018 FIVB Volleyball Women's World Championship in Japan held the banner together and shouted loudly, "Happy Birthday, Motherland!"

After stepping off the podium, the Chinese team received a congratulatory message from Chinese President Xi Jinping, which said, "In the matches, you were not afraid of strong opponents, dared to fight, showed your style and level and fully demonstrated the Chinese team's spirit of solidarity and hard work. I would like to extend warm congratulations and sincere greetings to you!"

On the night of winning the champion, the Chinese team returned to Beijing by a special plane to be received by Chinese President Xi Jinping at the Great Hall of the People. They were rewarded with the opportunity to take part in a series of celebrations for the National Day.

On October 1, the celebration of the 70th anniversary of the founding of the People's Republic of China was grandly held. In the float parade after the military parade, Lang Ping and other members of the Chinese team boarded the last float of the "Long Live the Motherland" square, holding

The Chinese women's volleyball team won the championship of the 13th FIVB Volleyball Women's World Cup, the best birthday present for their motherland. (Photo by Li Zhiyan)

flowers to greet the people.

This was Lang Ping's second appearance in the National Day celebration.

In 1984, Lang Ping, who had just won the gold medal at the Los Angeles Olympic Games with the Chinese team, stood on the float of the 35th National Day celebration with her teammates wearing the Olympic gold medals.

Thirty-five years had passed. Lang Ping, nicknamed the "Iron Hammer" once in her prime, was already in her late fifties. Once again wearing the gold medal on the National Day parade float, she demonstrated her long-term efforts and persistence that were really very touching.

When the float drove past Chang'an Street, the soldiers of the People's Liberation Army on the roadside neatly shouted, "Chinese Women's Volleyball Team, the world's No.1!" This was not only a great compliment to the new generation of women volleyball players, but also a salute to the generations of people who had devoted themselves to the cause of the Chinese women volleyball over the previous 40 years.

With the upcoming Tokyo Olympic Games, new challenges will be addressed by the Chinese team.

Off the podium, the Chinese women's volleyball team will start anew.

There will be no end to the unremitting efforts toward their cause.